Orchid Carousals

Lucy A. Snyder
with
Kaysee Renee Robichaud

Orchid Carousals

Lucy A. Snyder
with
Kaysee Renee Robichaud

CREATIVE GUY PUBLISHING
VICTORIA | CANADA

Orchid Carousals
Lucy A. Snyder
with Kaysee Renee Robichaud

Published in Canada by Creative Guy Publishing
Victoria, Canada
www.creativeguypublishing.com

ISBN 978-1894953-672
Trade paperback edition
Also published in Electronic Format

"Fall of Darkness" published in *Apocalypse Fiction* Magazine, July 2003.
"In The Wilderness" published in *Clean Sheets*, March 2001.
"Stripping in the Midwest" published in *Clean Sheets*, April 2003.

Acknowledgements

Writing is a solitary occupation, but making a book is not. I'd like to thank my first readers: Gary Braunbeck, Mark Freeman, Darien Cox, Trista Robichaud, and Scott Slemmons. I'd also like to thank Kaysee Renee Robichaud for her excellent story collaboration and Ursula Vernon for her wonderful cover art. And of course I'd like to thank Pete Allen for taking a risk by publishing something a bit outside CGP's usual genre range.

Contents

Part One:
Shimmer Stories

<u>At the Royal Orchid</u>

Part I: More

COOPER MARRON watched as the butch young waitress set a delicate cordial filled with a sparkling emerald liqueur down in front of the Warlock. "Compliments of the house, sir."

"Ooh! Pretty! Birthday dibs!" Jessie Shimmer reached across the pillaged Chinese food platters and snatched up the glass. She tossed the drink down as if it were a shot of vodka and set the emptied cordial between her two depleted old-fashioned glasses, both cloudy with the remains of White Russians. Cooper had shown her *The Big Lebowski* two weeks before, and she'd developed an amateur drinker's obsession with the libation.

"Mm, minty!" she remarked. "And sorta spicy. And...huh. What was in that, anyway?"

The waitress seemed stunned. "That—that drink wasn't for you, Miss."

Jessie grinned at her tipsily. "I'll buy him another."

Cooper cleared his throat beside her. "You left your purse at my apartment. Remember?"

"Oh. Yeah." She briefly looked embarrassed, but then she laid her head against his shoulder, batting her eyes at him. He could feel the heat of her warm cheek through the thin fabric of his grey Oxford shirt.

"So *you'll* buy him another?" she asked, her lips red and face flushed. The pilfered drink had turned her breath almost medicinally alcoholic. An absinthe cocktail? Whatever it was, he still had to resist the urge to lean down and kiss her. Resist, and resist: she was damn fine company, and plenty easy on the eyes, but really she was still just a kid. They could be friends, but that was as far as he could go.

Nothing more, he warned himself.

Cooper sighed exaggeratedly and smiled down at her. "Yes, I will buy him another."

He looked to the flustered waitress: "Another foofy green drink for my brother, please."

"But...there isn't any more." She anxiously rubbed a hand over her short dark pixie-punk cut, looking like she was going to cry. "There was just enough for one."

The Warlock held up his hands. "It's fine. Foofy green drinks aren't really my style, anyway. Just bring me another Märzen."

Still looking unhappy, the waitress left to fetch the Warlock a third bottle of his favored microbrew.

Jessie stifled a burp, shifted in her chair, then abruptly stood up, the chair legs scraping noisily on the floor. "I gotta go wee."

Cooper caught her by the arm as she lurched away from the table. "You need any help getting to the women's room?"

"No, I'm good. I haven't had *that* much to drink, sheez!" She smiled at him crookedly, then leaned down and kissed him on his cheek.

The sensation of her soft lips on his stubbly skin instantly made him go hard; he was glad for the cover the thick white napkin in his lap provided. He had never minded being naked in public, but he'd always felt embarrassed by unintentional erections. Probably because the Warlock had taken inordinate delight in giving him shit about them from the very first day that twelve-year-old Cooper woke up with morning wood, much to his then-six-year-old brother's amusement. As if being stuck in a tiny closet of a bedroom in the shabby foster home together hadn't been humiliating enough before that.

Cooper watched Jessie weave her way to the back of the Royal Orchid, then realized that staring at her butt in those tight jeans of hers was probably not the best way to get his woody to go down. He turned back to the table, and was met by his brother's smirk.

"So where did you find *that* one?" the Warlock asked.

"She was a student in my Introduction to Ubiquemancy class last quarter. But she's not my student any more. I haven't broken any OSU rules," Cooper replied, trying to keep his voice cool and casual.

"So what is she, like twenty-two or something?" The Warlock took a long draw from his beer mug.

"She's turning nineteen tonight."

The Warlock choked mid-swig and nearly spewed his brew. "Nine*teen*? You're dating a teenager?"

Cooper felt his cheeks grow hot, and vainly willed his heart to stop pounding. "She's well past the age of consent."

The Warlock cackled evilly and stomped the floor with his hobnail boots. He grabbed an empty beer bottle and used it as a pretend microphone for his best Billy Idol imitation: "Ow! Robbin' the cradle of lu-huuuve—"

"Dude, I'm not in the mood," Cooper said sharply.

"Aw, spoilsport." The Warlock put the bottle back on the table and was quiet for a moment. "So are you tapping that?"

Cooper clenched his fists under the table. "No. I'm not."

The Warlock stared at him for a moment. "Your dick okay, bro? They got pills for that now, you know—"

"Oh, you're *hilarious*. My dick is fine, but thanks oh so

—5—

much for your concern." Cooper frowned down at his half-empty Mai Tai. Normally he'd be on his fourth or fifth by now, but tonight he had to stay fit to drive. And liquor would surely weaken his resolve to keep his hands to himself.

"You should totally hit that," the Warlock continued. "You're already taking her out drinking; you shouldn't let that hot young pussy go to waste. I mean, you're what...thirty-four? You're practically old enough to be her *dad.* When are you gonna get thrown a bone like her again?"

Cooper closed his eyes and took a deep breath. *I will not punch my brother. I will not punch my brother. I will not punch my brother...*

The Warlock didn't seem to notice Cooper's rising anger and prattled on: "Nineteen-year-olds are good for exactly one thing, and it sure as hell ain't conversation. Everybody's gonna think you're doing her anyhow, so you might as well do her and have some fun in your life for once."

"We have fun," Cooper opened his eyes and fixed the Warlock in a glare. "I like just hanging out with her, watching movies and stuff."

"Seriously? You just...hang out and don't hook up?" The Warlock wore an expression of wide-eyed dismay. "Is *that* all I have to look forward to in my thirties? Pick up a girl at the club and then take her home so we can watch Netflix? *Pathetic.*"

"I like being around Jessie. She's nice." It was hard to put into words how he felt around the girl. He couldn't deny that he was incredibly attracted to her, but it was more than that. All his life, he'd felt a terrible dark pressure in the back of his mind, a looming sense of death and disaster. As a teenager the unrelenting stress of it had driven him to fight and drink and fuck, anything to drive the shadows away. And he hadn't stopped as an adult. He'd been with plenty of women, but what little peace he'd found in their company had only lasted as long as his orgasms.

It was different with Jessie. The darkness didn't leave when she was around, but it was...bearable. The world seemed like a friendlier, more livable place with her at his side. He didn't want to lose that. Didn't want to lose *her*. And maybe a tiny part of him feared that sex would irreparably taint things.

"*Nice*," the Warlock snorted. "Oh, *please*."

Cooper's resolution to not pound the ever-loving crap out of his brother was about to resoundingly break, but Jessie returned to the table and planted another kiss on his cheek. Just like that, his anger evaporated like aether. And he was once again glad for the cover of his napkin.

She plopped back down in her chair and grinned at them, her eyes glassy. It looked like the drinks were finally hitting her full-force. "You guys were talking about me, I can tell," she teased.

"Us? *Never*," the Warlock demurred as the waitress set down his fresh bottle of dark beer. "So what are you taking this quarter?"

"Um. Latin 2, Intro to Thaumaturgy, Egyptology, and hapkido. It's all pretty cool. I wish I could join the actual hapkido team, but I guess we're not allowed because we could have magical advantages or something. Which I don't get, 'cause we were allowed to compete in varsity sports in high school. But oh well."

While she was talking, she nonchalantly slipped her hand onto Cooper's thigh, lightly teasing his balls through his jeans with her pinkie. His pants were suddenly so tight it was hard to breathe.

She laid her head against his shoulder again. "I'm sleepy. Can you take me home?"

"Sure." The sooner he got her safely back to her dorm room, the sooner he could go someplace private and jack off. He pulled his wallet out of his back pocket and extracted three twenties. "That cover us?" Cooper asked his brother.

The Warlock nodded, his eyes sliding from Jessie to the empty cordial glass. "Looks fine to me. I think I'll hang in here a little longer and finish my beer."

They were barely outside before Jessie had snuck up behind him and stuck both her hands in the front pockets of his jeans, ticklishly fumbling around for his genitalia.

"Whoa! None of that, now!" He gently but firmly pulled her hands out of his pants.

"What? Don't you wanna?" She gazed up at him, her face flushed and moist with perspiration.

"I think you've had a little too much to drink." Cooper closed his eyes and spoke an ancient word for "sober", feeling the heat of the magic swell through him and flow out toward Jessie.

When he opened his eyes, Jessie was still looking at him, rosy-cheeked and now grinning. "Sobri'ty charms don' work on me. Mostly."

He stared down at her. "What? They don't?"

"Nuh uh. Madame Sagecroft tried for a whooooole hooour to get me sobered up after she caught us drinkin' in the lounge. I'm drunk as a skunk in a bunk until nature is as nature does."

Cooper chewed the corner of his moustache. "Look. I'm flattered. But no. If you're drunk, we can't do anything."

"Aw—"

"—And you're too young."

"*Bullshit!*"

Jessie argued with him as he half-dragged her to his car: a big, black, much-tinkered-with 1965 Lincoln Continental.

"I been fuckin' since I was fourteen!" she hollered, her Texas accent thickening as he bundled her into the wide leather passenger's seat. A couple of cooks taking a smoke break were staring at them from the kitchen entrance and whispering to each other. Great. So much for them ever coming *here* again without having to do a Walk of Shame. Cooper considered a silencing charm, but realized she'd never forgive him for that. Supposing she would forgive him for *this*. He could only hope she was so drunk she wouldn't remember.

"That's five whole years of fuckin'," she pleaded as he got into the driver's seat. "That's, like, a bachelor's degree in fuckin' and part of a Master's. I'm not too young. I'm *not*."

An image rose in Cooper's brain, unbidden, of Jessie riding some hot young stud on a bench in a high school locker room. In his mind's eye he could see her taut body rising and falling on the anonymous cock sliding smoothly within her tight flesh, her high breasts jiggling with each buck, her auburn hair thrown back and her face open in ecstasy.

"Look," he said, trying to sound as stern as possible. His erection was threatening to snap open the button on his jeans. "I think you're a great girl. I do. But I just don't feel right about this. I'm taking you home; please don't mess with me while I'm driving, okay?"

"'Kay. Whatever." Jessie crossed her arms tightly beneath her breasts and stared mournfully at her red Chuck Taylors.

He pulled out of the parking lot onto the highway. They drove back toward Columbus in silence, except for the occasional and somewhat ominous gurgle from Jessie's stomach. Was she going to get sick?

Jessie's eyes were fixed on a rapidly approaching side road. Her face was pinched and scarlet, as if she were suffering from some dire physical need. "Pull over. You gotta pull over."

Oh, hell. She was definitely going to be sick. He quickly turned right onto the road, which after a short leg through some dense trees opened into a small picnic area with a couple of concrete tables and barbecue grills. A single blue-white streetlight illuminated the empty park. Cooper pulled up near the concrete water fountain and killed the engine.

"So do you—" he began.

Jessie blurted out an old word for "naked" and suddenly her clothes were gone. In the next instant, she was on his lap, kissing him hard. And he was kissing her back, his hands on the velvety skin of her hips. She ground herself against his straining fly, her hard nipples pressed into his chest. He sucked at her pink tongue, tasting the mint, wormwood, honey and alcohol of her last drink, and beneath those tastes the kick of chili powder, the earthiness of rosemary, the bitterness of nettles...

He broke off the kiss, pulling away from her. "Wait. No. You took a potion."

"Mm." She started chewing on his neck.

"Jessie, listen! You're not thinking straight. You don't want this; it's just the potion making you do this."

Her hands had found his zipper and were tugging it down; in seconds her slim fingers were going to be on his naked shaft and he didn't think he had enough willpower left—

He quickly barked an old word for "flaccid". The magic felt like a punch in the nuts, but it did the job. His cock was down for at least a long eight count. Enough time to get her dressed and get them back on the road.

Jessie stared at him, looking horrified and deeply wounded. "Why did you do that? You really don't want me touching you? You don't want me, at all?"

"It's for your own good." The moment the words left his mouth, he felt like some ancient creaking relic who ought to be banging his walker on the floor, demanding that the nurse bring him his prune juice.

Pathetic, the Warlock sneered inside his head.

Her face darkened in what he first thought was embarrassment, but then her features twisted into rage and she grabbed the door's handle and pushed it open.

"Fuck this." She clambered off him, staggered onto the blacktop, and began to stride away, muttering complex and improbable obscenities under her breath. Part of him couldn't help but notice that her bare ass was just as amazing as he'd hoped it would be.

"Jessie, wait!" He fumbled with his zipper, got his pants closed, and hurried after her. "Where the heck are you going?"

"Back to the restaurant!" She quickened her pace.

"Why?"

"It's my damn birthday, and if you won't fuck me, I bet your brother will!"

Her threat was another punch to his tenders. The Warlock probably *would* fuck her, and do so without a drop of remorse if she showed up naked and profanely demanding his services as a cocksman, potion and booze be damned. It would be a clear case of waste not, want not in his brother's bloodshot eyes.

"Whoa, whoa, *whoa!*" He sprinted toward her and grabbed her elbow. "No, you just don't want to do that, *please!* Please come back to the car, okay?"

Jessie scowled at him for two heartbeats, but then her face crumpled and she started to weep. "I just wanted to have fun tonight. Why won't you touch me? I just want you to touch me."

The horned dilemma threatened to throw Cooper past being able to make a choice, and when he looked into her eyes and took in all that sadness and genuine pain, a dark voice in his head whispered to him that the gentlemanly thing to do would be to relieve what aches he could. If she'd skinned her knee, he'd smooth on a bandage. If she strained her shoulder, he'd give her a massage. Simple touch wasn't so wrong, was it?

He gave himself a harsh mental shake and pushed the voice away. *No.* He was creeping toward Creeperville. She was under the influence of a potion, and this had to stop. He closed his eyes, trying to steady himself, took a deep breath, and reached deeper into his well of magic. Under most circumstances, he'd have to brew an antidote potion to get all that out of her system, but maybe, just maybe, if he could summon the right spell...

The old, old words began spilling out of him, forgotten words for sobriety and purity and chastity, words that until now had no solid place in his mind or his vocabulary, and he felt the magic rise in him like a thousand celibate knights astride virginal white mares, thundering out of him in a bright, righteous lust-erasing wave straight at Jessie.

She let out a surprised gasp, and Cooper opened his eyes just in time to catch her before she fell backward onto the hard asphalt.

"Whoa! Jessie, are you okay?" He lowered her gently to the pavement, knelt beside her and patted her cheek. Was she unconscious? Maybe he'd gone too far.

She opened her eyes, looking disoriented. "What...what just happened?"

"Someone gave you a love potion. I cast a spell to get rid of it."

Her expression switched from raw confusion to an embarrassment that bordered on panic. "Why am I naked?"

"You charmed your clothes off; don't you remember?"

She shook her head, biting her lip anxiously. "No. I feel like I've been sleepwalking or something and just woke up."

"You're fine," he replied gently. "You probably didn't send

your clothes very far; it didn't feel like you used enough magic for that. There's nobody around. C'mon, let's go find them and we can get you home, okay?"

He helped her to her feet and they began to scour the bushes bordering the picnic area. Cooper focused on the search and tried not to look at her naked body. Her nipples were getting hard in the cool spring night air. Jessie seemed to notice his averted gaze, and by her increasingly dismayed expression, he figured she thought he was ashamed of her. And he didn't know how to comfort her. He didn't know what to tell her in mundane, everyday words that wouldn't sound ridiculous or stupid. Everything suddenly seemed impossibly awkward.

They found her tee shirt in a yew bush after a couple of minutes, and she quickly slipped it on, pulling it down as far as it would go, as if simple tugging could somehow make it cover her entire body. Cooper briefly wondered if performing a fabric extension charm would be prudent, but then Jessie spotted her jeans and red satin underwear draped across one of the concrete tables.

"Oh, good, they didn't get muddy!" She hurried over, slipped into the whisper-thin thong, and shook out her Levis. A small square blue packet flipped out of one of the front pockets and fell onto the concrete bench. Jessie paused, stared down at it for a moment, and then slowly picked it up with a trembling hand.

"What's the matter?" Cooper stepped toward her.

"It wasn't because of the potion. It wasn't because I was drunk." Blushing, but no longer looking embarrassed, she held the royal blue packet out to him on her outstretched palm as if it were some precious magical key she'd just discovered.

It was a lubricated Trojan condom.

"I was stone sober when I put this in my pocket," she said. "I put it there hoping that if things went well, you would make love to me tonight. Because I've wanted you since the first moment I saw you standing at the whiteboard in your tight khakis and black sweater. I got Cs on those first two pop-quizzes you gave us because all I could think about was wondering what you looked like naked, and wondering what it would feel like to have your hands all over me."

"Jessie, I—" he began.

She tossed the condom on the table, grabbed him by his shoulders and pulled his head to hers so she could kiss him, hard, her tongue sliding between his teeth into his mouth. His erection resurrected with a sharp, hungry throb. And then she was pushing him down onto the concrete bench, straddling his lap.

"Touch me," she whispered hoarsely in his ear. "I swear to God I'm sober now and I'm old enough and I want you and please touch me."

She pulled her tee shirt off over her head, her lovely pink nipples crinkling in the cool air. Cooper took the left one in his mouth. She sucked in her breath and arched her back, dropping her shirt onto the concrete slab. Her hips rose from his lap, and he pressed two fingers against the strip of satin covering the cleft of her close-trimmed vulva.

"Ah! Yes. More." She rose up further so she could shimmy her thong halfway down her thighs, and then she lowered herself, leaning into his hand. Her flesh was tremendously swollen, and wet. The sweet-salty smell of her began to fill the air, and he felt his cock go as hard as it had ever been, his balls aching for release. He ran his middle finger up the slick groove of her labia and found her clit.

Jessie let out a tiny moan and squeezed her eyes shut. "Yes. There. Please."

He began to circle her clit with his finger, slowly, gently, and she gripped his shoulders, her eyes still closed, her lips parted in anticipation. He reached behind her with his left hand so he could tease the opening of her vagina. Within just a few seconds, a shudder ran through her, and he felt her flesh begin to contract, seemingly eager to draw his fingers inside, and as she came she let out another wail that threatened to deafen him.

"Oh god." She opened her eyes and stared at him, her expression intense. "You need to fuck me, Mister Marron. But not here. This concrete bench is gonna take the skin right off my knees."

Jessie pressed the Trojan into his hand and led him back to his Lincoln. She sat on the wide black hood, still toasty from the heat of the engine, grabbed him by the waistband of his jeans and pulled him close. They kissed as she unbuttoned his gray oxford, and once his shirt was off she began licking his right nipple as she unzipped his jeans.

Cooper sucked in his breath as she pulled his cock out of his boxer briefs, exposing his aching flesh to the evening chill. Grinning, Jessie slid off the hood of the car, leaned down, and began to suck him.

"Jesus, Jessie," he gasped. The sensation of her lips and tongue across his shaft was intense, too intense, and he could feel himself rocketing perilously close to orgasm. "Wait, stop, you're gonna make me come—"

He tried to push her back, just so he could get a grip on himself and think about toads or cleaning charms or something else to cool himself off so he could last at least somewhat longer than a horny high school boy, but she gripped his hips with both hands and drove his cock straight down her hot throat. And he was coming in a sweet, hard rush, and she was drinking his semen down like it was another White Russian.

"Jesus." Cooper tried to blink away the spots in his vision. And then he had a moment of worry that after his earlier charm he'd done himself a mischief and wouldn't be able to rise again to satisfy the girl. But Jessie had pulled his jeans and underwear down to his ankles and now she was teasing his balls with her nimble fingers, circling the point of her tongue over the sensitive frenulum at the base of his cockhead, and within a minute he was hard again. She took the Trojan from his hand, expertly ripped open the wrapper with her teeth, and rolled the slippery condom onto his shaft.

He awkwardly kicked out of his trousers and shoes while Jessie lay back on the hood of the car. Her vulva was beautiful, slick and open like a night-blooming flower. He stepped up to the car, pulled her closer to him, and leaned down so he could kiss her lovely breasts. She gripped his sheathed cock and guided him home. He pushed into her slowly, gently at first; her flesh was tight, and seemed unusually warm, as if some secret fire burned in her core. But she was so, so wet, and his cock seemed to fit inside her perfectly.

"Harder." She wrapped her legs around his hips and bucked against him. "I want you to fuck me hard. I won't break, trust me."

Cooper obliged, plunging himself inside her, and with each uninhibited thrust the darkness in his mind fled. All he could feel was her heat, all he could hear was her voice gasping in his ear, all he could see was the light shining in her hazel eyes. For a moment his heart caught in his chest, and he wondered if he might die, and in the next moment he realized he wouldn't mind so much if this wonderful, peaceful ecstasy was the end of him.

But he didn't die, and the girl gave a hoarse moan as she came again, her inner muscles gripping his cock powerfully. The delicious sensation tipped him over the edge and he was coming too, a shock of joy that felt like a lightning bolt piercing him from the top of his head to the soles of his feet.

His vision went white, and it was only the embrace of her strong legs that kept him from falling backward.

When he could see again, he crawled up onto the hood and held her close in his quivering arms.

"That was amazing," he whispered, feeling as if something inside him had been stripped clean and bare.

I can't lose this, he thought, hugging Jessie closer. *I can't lose her.*

She ran her fingers through his sweaty curls and laughed, her voice husky and satiated. "Yes, it was."

They lay there on the shiny dark metal, cuddling in blissful silence, until Jessie stirred restlessly.

"Huh. You know what doesn't make any sense?" she asked.

"What?" he replied.

"The Warlock...I took his drink. The potion was supposed to be *his*. Why in the heck would anyone give a hornball like him a libido booster?"

Nobody would, unless...unless they wanted him to have sex with someone he'd never touch of his own free will. And Cooper was stumped to imagine who that could possibly be. His mind flashed back on the time he'd found the Warlock getting a blowjob from a minotaur in the back of a biker bar. And the time he found him in a siren's embrace at a pool party. The creature behind the potion would have to be someone truly hideous. More than just hideous, *monstrous*. Something that wasn't even close to human.

"Oh, hell," Cooper said. "He could be in serious trouble."

"What should we do?"

"We better go back to the restaurant and get him out of there," he replied. "I've got a shotgun and a couple of pistols in the trunk of my car if things look bad. But first let's find the rest of your clothes..."

Part II: Party

After Cooper helped his drunken girl up from the table and out the door, the Warlock's eye once again fell on the empty cordial glass. He lifted it, sniffed it. And recognized it immediately.

The waitress who'd given it to him was nowhere in sight. Smirking at the thought of what Jessie was doing to Cooper that very moment, the Warlock pushed away from the table, carried the glass with him to the men's room and stared at it while he got rid of his spent beer. Then he sauntered over to the bar where the restaurant's owner Aileen Cheng was tidying up for the evening.

"Last call, darlin'?" Aileen smiled at him; she had a touch of her mother's Scottish brogue, and the Warlock had always found her accent incredibly sexy. Along with the rest of her. She had the kind of ripe curves he'd always wanted to run his tongue along. Although they'd flirted plenty, she'd never done anything but smile at his suggestions that they go someplace quiet and have a little fun together.

"Where's my waitress?" he asked, holding up the cordial glass.

"Joey? She said she wasn't feeling well and went on break." She frowned. "Did she mess up your order?"

"She gave me this. On the house, she said."

Aileen peered at the green liquor that filmed the glass, then took it from him and sniffed it.

"A little Love Potion Number Nine?" he asked. "I didn't know this was on the bar menu."

"It's most certainly not." Her frown deepened into genuine anger for a moment, but then a realization seemed to dawn, and in the next second she looked both exasperated and amused. "Oh. I know *exactly* what this is about. I'm so sorry."

"Care to share?" he asked.

"It's...complicated." She combed her fingers through her thick black hair. "She should tell you herself. She means well, but...well, this shite isn't cool at all. You don't give somebody a potion like this without his permission. You just don't. She needs to apologize to you."

The Warlock drew a circle in the air around his face with his index finger. "This isn't me looking mad, okay? I didn't drink it; my brother's date did."

"Oh no, is she okay?"

"She'll be fine; Coop's a big boy, and he can take care of her."

Aileen called one of the cooks out of the kitchen to finish cleaning up for her, and then she took off her apron and led the Warlock to the secluded door that opened onto the stairs down to her basement apartment. Which he certainly hadn't imagined he'd finally be visiting tonight.

Curiouser and curiouser, he thought.

He'd seen his share of apartments above and below restaurants; they were usually cramped, messy places, courtesy of the occupants spending most of their lives tending bar and cooking and not having much time for niceties such as reorganizing and vacuuming. But Aileen's place, despite being buried completely underground, was clean, airy, and well-lit. The walls were a fashionable tan marble, and the ceiling was dotted with domed light tubes that he figured routed sunshine in during the day. To his left was a sitting area with a black leather couch and a couple of matching chairs; to the right, a kitchenette and wet bar. In the back he could see a door leading to a dimly-lit bedroom, and beside it a door that led to a spacious, well-lit luxury bathroom with a curbless marble shower stall.

And tucked into the far right-hand corner of the room,

he saw a purple-curtained alcove containing a single bed outfitted in matching purple satin sheets. Somebody—the Warlock guessed it was Joey, since the waitress was sitting on the lonely mattress with her head in her hands—had scrawled an assortment of pictures and graffiti on the wall with a dark artist's crayon or charcoal pencil.

"Hey Joey." Aileen raised the cordial glass. "Explain yourself."

The startled waitress looked up, and the color drained from her face. She jumped to her feet, made an awkward jerk as if she wanted to run away, but clearly she'd already fled to the one place she could think to hide in. The Warlock hadn't really looked at her before; she was pretty, in an androgynous way, and young. Not *too* young, probably, but certainly younger than he was. Jessie gave the impression of being older than this girl, but the faint worry lines on Joey's forehead told a different story.

"I...I." Her voice failed as she stared at the Warlock, embarrassed pink slowly blossoming on her cheeks.

"If you liked me, all you had to do was tell me," he replied, stepping toward her. "You know, talk to me a little? Instead of giving me a spiked drink?"

Her blush deepened to a mortified red.

"I'm sorry, I j-just..." she stammered.

"Just what?" he asked, not unkindly.

She started shaking her head. "You wouldn't want somebody like me. You *wouldn't*. I—I've been watching you for months, and all the girls and the boys say you're so good, but...you wouldn't want me. I'm a *freak*."

A freak? Really? He looked her up and down. She had two slim legs he thought would fit nicely around his waist, two well-toned arms, two pretty brown eyes, ten slender fingers with no nails to catch on sensitive flesh, a nice double-handful of breasts, no fur or fangs or scales in sight...what could be so different underneath her black restaurant polo and jeans that she'd apparently come to believe she was so utterly undesirable? He felt his cock stir along with his curiosity.

Aileen sighed. "Joey, darlin', we've talked about this. You're not a freak, you're just *fine*." She walked past the Warlock and gave the girl a long, affectionate hug. "You're fine, baby. But you shouldn't have done that."

A couple of tears dripped down Joey's cheeks. "I know. I'm sorry. I won't ever do it again, I swear."

Aileen kissed her on the lips. The Warlock had seen many platonic, sisterly kisses between women; this was not one of them. He went fully hard at the charged look they gave each other as they broke off their embrace.

"How old are you?" the Warlock asked the girl.

"Twenty-two. In th-three days."

"Have you ever been with anybody besides Aileen?"

The girl stared down at her shoes and shook her head, turning even redder.

"Do you want me to make love to you?" he asked.

She met his gaze, finally, her jaw tightening a bit.

"Yes." Her voice was steadier. "But not if it's just going to be a pity fuck."

"No. It won't be. Pity doesn't get me hard. They'd have never let me volunteer at the greyhound rescue center if it did." He dug in his pocket and pulled out a small quartz crystal carved in the shape of a phallus. "Please hold out your hand."

When she stared at the fetish and didn't move, he added, "I promise this won't hurt or anything. Just hold out your hand."

Joey didn't budge.

"Oh, for goodness...here, let me show you." Aileen held out her own hand. "Do me first so she can see."

The Warlock took the woman's hand and pressed tip of the crystal against her wrist. The phallus flashed a quick series of green; her body was clear of sexually transmitted diseases. She wasn't infected with vampirism or lycanthropy, either. In fact, she didn't even have so much as a head cold.

"See?" Aileen withdrew her hand. "Nothing bad will happen."

Joey finally did as he asked. He took her hand, planted a kiss on her palm, and pressed his fetish against her thumb. It flashed all green. Well then. He cleared his throat, catching Aileen's attention, and raised his eyebrows at her, giving her an *Are you sure you're cool with this?* look.

Aileen shrugged and smiled as if to say, *Sure, if it'll get this out of her system.* But there was a certain dirty gleam in her eye that made him pretty damn sure she wasn't doing this purely for Joey's sake.

The Warlock smiled at the girl.

"So what do you want for your early birthday present?" he purred in his best come-sit-on-Santa's-lap voice.

"Um." She licked her lips, staring at the bulge in his jeans. "Strip for me."

"Okay...but only if you promise to let me take *your* clothes off afterward."

She nodded, her eyes huge.

"I should go latch the doors," Aileen announced, sweeping back toward the stairs, "just to make sure nobody wanders down here and walks in on us."

The Warlock pulled off his hobnail boots—he was secretly glad he was wearing dark socks that matched—and then slowly began to peel out of his Black Label Society tee shirt. Once his furry, muscular chest was bared, he unbuckled his stiff leather belt, pulling it slowly from the loops on his black jeans. He tossed the belt aside—but not too far away in case the girl wanted to bind him with it—and pulled a silver cigarette case out of the back pocket of his jeans. And then he unzipped himself. His boxer briefs weren't anything fancy, just a black pair of Calvins, but the fabric was soft and people seem to think they looked good on him.

He stepped out of his jeans and walked over to Joey, who was sitting at rapt attention on the edge of her bed. "I thought you might want to do the last part yourself."

She paused, then took hold of his waistband with both hands and slowly eased the underwear down his body, staring at his naked cock with an expression of mixed awe and lust. And maybe just a bit of "Will that all fit?" worry at the edges.

"Holy chipotle." Aileen had ninjaed back from the stairs and was standing to his right, staring at him with unvarnished appreciation. "Carlos wasn't exaggerating about you, was he?"

He arched an eyebrow at Aileen. "I know a spell to make it more petite if you like."

"No," Joey said. "I don't want it smaller."

"Fabulous." He leaned down and gave her a kiss. She seemed startled at first, but then she returned the kiss, slipping her soft tongue into his mouth. Her hair smelled like fried wontons. He lifted her up from the bed and undid her apron strings, then pulled her black polo up over her head. She had an intricate tattoo of a vine of purple orchids on the right side of her back; the tattoo disappeared under her jeans. He wondered how far down it went.

Joey quivered a little but didn't object as he undid her bra; her breasts were firm and high. He flicked his tongue over her left nipple, and she sucked in her breath. But when he moved down to her hips, a look of terror crossed her face, and she grabbed his hands to stop him.

"What's the matter?" he asked.

"I—I..." Joey trailed off, looking desperately at Aileen, who had quietly zipped out of her black work dress and was slipping down her silk stockings. The Warlock took a half-second to admire her purple silk bra and panties before he turned his attention back to Joey.

"You're fine, darlin'." Aileen stepped up beside them and took the girl's hand. "You don't have anything to be ashamed of. Honest."

"If you want me to stop, I'll stop," he told Joey. "But I gotta say, you got me curious. I'd really like to see you."

She closed her eyes and swallowed, and for the first time he noticed the slightest rise of cartilage in her throat. "Okay. You can see me if you want."

He moved his hands to her fly...and realized he felt a definite phallic bump beneath. Was she wearing a pack-and-play toy? That certainly wasn't anything to feel freakish about. He knew at least three women who were into gender play and regularly strapped on silicone cocks beneath their clothes. It wasn't a big deal. He unzipped her pants and pulled down her blue boxers, expecting to see a flesh-colored dildo pop up like a carnal jack-in-the-box—

—and instead found himself staring a small, cute, but unmistakably real penis.

It was slender and pink and maybe five inches long; even as rock-hard as it clearly was, it carried an illusion of softness. Joey's dick was probably the most adorable thing he'd seen in six months; he managed to catch himself right before he went "Awww" at it like it was a kitten or puppy. Cocks, even extremely cute ones, were to be treated with respect. Particularly on a first date.

So, she's transitioning from male to female. Still not even close to a big deal, he thought as he pulled her pants and shorts down her slender, hairless legs. And then as he knelt before her, he got a good look at the rest of her genitalia. Her walnut-sized balls were covered in fine pale fuzz instead of a dark thatch of pubic hair. Her scrotum separated and melded into labia. His heart beat a little faster when realized she had a vagina. Which, despite her trembling, was very wet. She smelled pleasantly like soy sauce.

"This is so cool," he said.

"See?" Aileen gave Joey a side hug. "You didn't have a thing to worry about."

The Warlock looked up at the girl. "The next time you want to seduce a guy like me? Skip the potion. Just sidle up to him and whisper 'Wanna come see my dick?' And give him a smile. Trust me. That's all you'll need to do."

She stared down at him with a look of disbelief. "You're kidding, right?"

He shook his head. "Not a bit."

"Well, I don't think that line would work on *every* man," Aileen countered with a slight disapproving frown. "Or even most, really. In fact, that would be bloody dangerous in your average biker bar."

"Yeah, but saying that would totally work on *me*. And that's what's important, right?" He winked broadly at both of them.

Aileen rolled her eyes, but smiled just the same.

The Warlock stood and held up the silver cigarette case. "Well, I've got some packets of lube, and a couple of different brands of ultra-thin condoms in here if you wanted to fuck me for a while. You might like the Kimonos."

Joey's look of amazement was priceless. "You want me to fuck you?"

"Well, I don't bottom for just *anyone*," he replied. "But seeing as it's your birthday, I say it's your party, and your choice."

She grabbed him by the head and pulled him in for a kiss. A moment later, Aileen was kissing him too, and the sensation of their hands and nipples brushing all over his body was amazing. Threesomes were beautiful when the chemistry was right, and the chemistry here was feeling better and better.

Smiling, Aileen led them both back to her room, which held a much better playground: a king-sized bed with a green satin comforter and sheets. The Warlock noticed that Joey's orchid tattoo crossed over her hips and went almost all the way down the back of her left leg.

"I want you to go down on her," Joey whispered in his ear, "while I do you from behind."

"Sounds fun," he murmured back, "but shouldn't we check with your girlfriend first to see if she wants that?"

"Check with me about what?" Aileen asked as she shimmied out of her underwear and climbed onto the bed.

"You wanna be pillow queen?" Joey asked.

Aileen clapped with joy. "Always!"

The Warlock crawled onto the bed after her on his hands and knees and began kissing his way up the insides of her legs as he listened to Joey rip open various packets behind him.

"Oh, wow, you waxed back here," she said, running a lubed finger down his smooth crack to his balls.

"As it turns out," he said between gentle nibbles on Aileen's thighs, "hair taco just wasn't a very popular menu item."

Aileen giggled at that, but her laughter melted into sighs as he breathed on her nicely-furred vulva and ran his tongue over her lips. He loved the tangy flavor of a woman's juice; he couldn't wait to do this to Joey later. Did Joey have a prostate *and* a G-spot? Lord, he was going to enjoy making her scream. But he needed to focus on the woman at hand; he and Joey would have all night to explore each other. And maybe the next morning, too, if she wasn't needed on the early lunch shift.

He slipped his tongue into Aileen's sweetness, and Joey

pushed against his tight ring, sliding her lubed finger into him. He shivered as she drizzled cold lube from the packet onto his flesh, working it inside him little by little. His cock was almost painfully hard now; he'd have loved to plunge it into the soft warmth his tongue was probing. But there would be time for that, too.

Joey pressed her cock against him; she hesitated for a moment, then gripped his thighs with her hands and drove herself in with a moan. His flesh burned exquisitely around hers; she felt a whole lot bigger now that she was inside him.

"Don't be shy," he said, coming up for air. "Go as fast or as slow as you want."

The one downside to being fucked while he was going down on another person, he thought, was the distraction factor. The closer he got to his own orgasm, the sloppier he inevitably got with the person he was devouring. He didn't know if Aileen was the kind of woman who had multiple orgasms or not, but he wanted to make sure he got her off with honors at least once before he was too far gone to do a decent job. And as hot as this was, he was pretty sure he'd come from Joey's enthusiastic rogering even if neither of the women actually touched his cock.

"Be nice to our guest and give him a reacharound, darlin'," Aileen prompted.

"Oh. Yeah. Right," Joey panted. She slipped the hand that she hadn't used to lube him up around his waist and began to squeeze and stroke him.

Hells bells. He was going to come a whole lot quicker than he'd planned. Best to not beat around the bush any longer, then. He slipped two fingers inside Aileen, quickly finding the swollen wrinkles of her G-spot, and began to suck on her clit.

"Oh my!" she gasped. "You've done this a time or two,

haven't you?"

He continued to work at the nubbin of flesh, and he felt her inner wrinkles smooth as her g-spot swelled, a little pillow of fluid. When her dam broke, he knew she was going to get juice all over him, and he'd love every second of it.

"Ah, I can't stand it," Aileen moaned, pushing his hands away. "I need you to fuck me."

"Fuck her," Joey said, breathless. "Hurry."

She let him up long enough for Aileen to slide herself into place beneath him. The Warlock grabbed a condom from his case and put it on in record time. Aileen gave a little cry as he entered her, and a second later Joey was penetrating him again, and it took them a couple of seconds to find a good rhythm, but once they found it, oh, it was sweet, it was better than chocolate cake and ice cream and Joey was fucking him as hard as she could, and he was pounding himself into Aileen, and he could feel all the muscles in her body winding tighter and tighter and she was so, so close and so was he—

Aileen threw her head back against the mattress and wailed and a half second later Joey was speaking in tongues behind him and he felt her cock jump inside him as Aileen's flesh clamped down on him and he was coming so hard that he was half-expecting to pass out and have some kind of out-of-body experience.

They all collapsed in a sweaty heap and lay there like dead people.

"That was great," Aileen finally said. "But the two of you are kinda heavy."

"I can't move until Joey moves," he replied.

"I can't feel my legs," she said.

And just then, the door to the apartment got kicked down with a loud bang, and Jessie and Cooper rushed in. Cooper was holding a .38 pistol in one hand and a ball of green flame in the other, and Jessie gripped a Mossberg shotgun.

The Warlock winced. Joey squeaked in alarm and curled up tight against his back, hiding her face against his shoulder. Aileen just blinked and stared at the interlopers.

"Stand down, hellbeast!" Cooper shouted. The ball in his hand flared high. "Release my brother or feel my wrath!"

"Jesus H. Christ," the Warlock shouted back. "Who are you two supposed to be, Starsky and Cockblock?"

Cooper lowered his pistol and hurried toward the bedroom. "Are you okay? We thought you were—oh."

His brother's eyes widened as he looked from Joey to Aileen and then back to the Warlock. A smile played on his lips. "You're, uh...you're fine then, huh?"

"As you can see, I am the meat in a girl sandwich," the Warlock replied. "And if you do not wish to be on the receiving end of a knuckle sandwich, please leave. *Now*. And fix the door on your way back out."

"Yeah. We'll do that." Cooper was grinning like a loon as he backed up. "Sorry, ladies! See you around, huh?"

"Knuckle. Sandwich!"

"Leaving now!"

The Warlock heard Cooper utter an impromptu spell from the stairs and saw a green flash as the door was restored.

Joey gave a sigh of relief, stretched and rolled off the Warlock. He in turn got to his knees and helped Aileen sit up.

"Well, that was...unexpected," she said. "I hope they didn't break down any of my other doors."

"I'm sure they'll take care of any damage on their way out." He twisted, popping his spine pleasantly, and pulled off the spent condom. "So who's up for round two in the shower?"

"Me!" Joey and Aileen exclaimed simultaneously.

Best. Birthday Party. Ever, he thought with a smile.

Demonized

MOTHER KAREN Mercedes Sebastián was in the kitchen showing her 17-year-old foster son Jimmy how to make a quick healing poultice from simple kitchen herbs when her tertiary intruder alarm went off.

"There's a demon in the house!" the spell's high voice exclaimed inside her head. "A war minion of Aži Dahāka is in your study!"

The knife fell from her hand and clattered onto the maple cutting board.

"Mother Karen, are you all right?" Jimmy asked, concerned.

She shook her head, holding up her hand for silence, listening. None of the other alarm spells had gone off. If a demon had set a single claw on the roof or the front lawn of the rambling Old Worthington colonial, a dozen other defensive spells would have engaged. *Should* have, anyhow.

The twenty children in her care all had varying forms of magical talents, and her kids were attractive targets to most any malevolent spirit that existed in the universe. Some would want to lure them away and use the young Talents to increase their power; others would want to defile something tender and pure. And still others simply wanted a tasty snack. Mother Karen had been acutely aware of this reality from the very beginning, and she had enlisted the very best enchanters to protect the foster home.

How was it possible that an entity—a soldier demon, no less—had gotten itself into her study without triggering any of the other spells? It couldn't have simply manifested itself in there, could it?

Fear was congealing into a cold lump in the pit of her stomach. She closed her eyes, concentrating. None of the kids were in the bedrooms near her study. That was a fortunate turn, at least.

"Mother Karen?" Jimmy asked again.

"We have a serious problem," she whispered back. "Come with me."

She led Jimmy to the hallway coat closet where she kept a small but effective cache of weapons. The door hidden in the rear wall of the closet silently slid open at her touch, and the items she sought fell into her hands without her having to hunt for them.

"Take these." She handed Jimmy a simple but effective gold-and-mahogany disintegration wand and the emergency cell phone. "The trigger word for the wand is printed on the side. You know how to pronounce Russian, right?"

He nodded, his eyes huge. "What's going on?"

"There's something in the house that shouldn't be here. I want you to get Jodi and Michael and have them help you get everyone down to the playroom in the basement. Lock the doors behind you. Wait in there for me to give the all-clear. If—"

Mother Karen took a deep breath. "If you hear an alarm in your head that I've died, take it seriously; if you see someone that looks like me after that, it won't be. The moment that death alarm goes off, or if you hear an alarm that I've been bound, call the first number in this phone—it'll connect you right to the Governing Circle's paranormal defense team. They'll know to get here ASAP. Try to be as calm if you can; the little ones won't hear the alarms as long as you and Jodi and Michael are around."

"What if something gets into the playroom?" the boy asked.

"If the thing gets to you before the team does, blast it with the wand and keep blasting it. Don't let up even if it begs for mercy."

"W-why don't we just call the Circle right now?" Jimmy looked as scared as she'd ever seen him in the six years he'd lived under her roof.

"This is our house, and our job to protect it," she replied. "If the monsters out there see us calling for help over every little thing that happens, they'll figure we're weak, and they'll come at us that much harder."

She paused, considering the horrified look the boy was giving her, and tousled his hair affectionately. "We'll be fine. Just do your part and keep the other kids calm and quiet. This isn't my first demon, and I don't plan to die tonight, okay?"

Once Jimmy left to collect the other children, Mother Karen ducked back into the closet to select her own weapon. She had over two dozen wands, staves, and various types of enchanted swords and guns.

Aži Dahāka was old-school evil, and his war minions generally weren't a subtle bunch. She didn't have anything specific to his pantheon, but...yes. Her hand fell upon a silver staff, the metal wrought to look like an oaken branch. The staff was topped with a smooth, three-inch orb of amber. The hardened sap contained three twined hairs from the goddess Andraste, who had inspired her people to victory with the power of a mother's righteous vengeance. Perfect.

The door to her study was closed and locked, just as she'd left it. But she could feel the dark thrumming of some powerful presence behind the sturdy wood. The hairs on her arms rose along with her fear. She swallowed it down, got a better grip on the staff, and opened the door, expecting to find her study wrecked or on fire.

But the room was fine. A demoness stood at the shelves by Karen's computer, slowly paging through an old spellbook. She was a pallid, subterranean thing; her albino vulture wings were stained with soot and old blood, and her kilt, boots, and jacket were rough-stitched from the shed skins of giant serpents. The belt at her hips supported a sheathed black steel scimitar.

Mother Karen raised the staff to blast the demon, but something about the set of her shoulders and her stance was oddly familiar, and the white witch stayed her hand.

The demoness turned toward Karen, fixed her in a steady gaze with her watery purple eyes, and smiled, her pale lips skinning away from sharp iron-black teeth. "Hey there, Kare-Bear. How's it been?"

Only one person in her whole life had called her that silly name. It had been over thirty years since she'd heard it. The room seemed to spin, and Karen had to lean hard against her staff to keep from wobbling.

"Veronica?"

"In the flesh. Or what passes for it these days." The demoness laughed the same way Veronica used to laugh when Karen beat her at cards, and suddenly so many old memories were flooding back that Karen had to steady herself again.

She hadn't heard anything from or about Veronica since the night of their last confrontation at college. Karen had caught Veronica vivisecting a rat for some piece of necromancy. *Again*, after Veronica had promised a dozen times to stop dabbling in the dark arts. They fought, Veronica stormed out and never came back. Probably a million college romances had broken just the same way. After a month of silence, Karen had vowed to forget her girlfriend and move on with her life. And she'd surely moved on. But the forgetting had never quite happened. When Karen pleasured herself on lonely nights, Veronica's body was the one she summoned in her fantasies.

"So did you heal that rat?" Veronica closed the spellbook and carefully slid it back into its place on the shelf.

Karen nodded. "I let it go near the river."

Her demon ex-girlfriend laughed again, and Karen thought her heart would break at the sound.

"That's my Kare-Bear," Veronica said, sounding wistful rather than scornful. "Rescuer of all creatures great and small. It must do your heart a world of good to see me like this, eh? To know that all your dread predictions about my future, all the warnings you gave me that I cheerfully blew off, were right on target?"

"It does my heart no good whatsoever to see you like this," Karen replied faintly. "What happened to you?"

"Jesus. What *didn't* happen to me, you know? But this new gig?" Veronica touched the iron choker chain that marked her as a supernatural slave. "I lost half my soul in a bad poker bet, if you can believe it."

Karen shook her head. "You were always the worst bluffer."

The demoness chuckled bitterly. "Yeah. That's always been the flaw in my grand plans."

"How did you get in here?"

"Through there." Veronica pointed at the huge mirror above the enchanted fireplace.

Karen frowned. "How? I have a dozen spells protecting that from hellions."

Veronica waved a taloned finger at her in mock admonishment. "You once told me I was always welcome in your home. And you never took back that invitation. You should probably check to make sure that none of your other girlfriends ended up like me."

"I'd think you'd be the only one."

"Oh really? You seemed to like us shady types pretty well; I wouldn't be too surprised if you had another ex or two in hell."

Veronica moved toward her, and the sudden scent of serpent offal, brimstone and battlefield charnel set Karen's heart pounding with fear again.

"Don't take another step." Karen pointed the staff at the demoness. She couldn't quite keep her hand from shaking. "What do you want here?"

"I don't have any interest in your foster kids or in screwing up your nice suburban witch life," Veronica replied. "But I got word that I've been 'specially chosen' for a certain quest I can't say much about, and...yeah. I'm gonna die. Soon. And I thought, okay, I have an evening of relative freedom before the inevitable...what do I want? I thought about it, and I realized that what I wanted more than anything else in the universe was to make love to you just one last time. Or die trying."

Karen's lips worked a moment before she got any words out. "You can't be serious."

"I'm completely serious." Veronica unbuckled her sword belt and let the leather-sheathed scimitar fall to the floor with a thud.

"You're crazy," Karen said.

"But you always liked that about me, didn't you?" Veronica winked and undid the laces on her jacket. When the demoness shrugged out of the grey serpent skins, Karen couldn't take her eyes off her breasts. They'd changed, pale as the rest of her now with black aureoles, but they were still high and firm. Karen wondered if they'd taste the same, or if they'd be bitter with rust and sulfur now.

Veronica slipped out of her snakey kilt, and Karen sucked in her breath at the sight of her naked vulva. She'd dreamed about Veronica on so many nights, but not like *this*. Her duty to her home and her foster children told her that Veronica had made her own bad choices, twisted herself, and now she deserved to be blown out of her stinking boots like any other demon. But what if Veronica had come here not to harm, not to debase, but to seek redemption? Could Karen live with herself if she coldly slaughtered the remorseful demon who used to be the girl she'd loved more than anyone else?

Karen shook her head, her knuckles white around the silver staff. "I couldn't possibly. No."

"Just one kiss, then." Veronica stepped forward, naked but for her boots and iron collar, and Karen couldn't find the voice to stop her. "One kiss won't hurt, will it?"

The white witch found herself lowering the staff as the demoness came closer, and before the holy relic could touch and burn her visitor, Karen let it fall to the plush cream-colored carpet. And then, before her fear could find its voice again, she grabbed Veronica's shaved head and pulled her down for a kiss.

The demoness made a surprised, happy noise as Karen slipped her tongue into her sharp-toothed mouth, tasting brimstone and death, yes, but beneath that was the flavor of the girl she still remembered, still loved deep in a place she'd hidden from herself, and that suddenly-realized love, brought out into the firelight of her secluded haven, blossomed into a lust she hadn't felt in years. It was exhilarating.

If Veronica tries to take a step outside this room, I'll do what's necessary, Karen thought, trying to soothe her own guilty feelings that she was abdicating her responsibilities in the most appalling way. But as long as the demoness stayed where she was...yes. Karen realized she didn't mind satisfying her old girlfriend's final request. She didn't mind it at all.

Veronica grabbed double-handfuls of Karen's hair and pulled her head back so she could lick Karen's neck. Karen moaned, sliding her hands down to the demoness' hips, squeezing the firm ass she'd dreamed of on a thousand dark nights.

"I can smell you. I can smell your pussy getting very, very wet right now," Veronica whispered, her voice every bit the voice of the dangerous creature she'd become. And if anything, Karen's desire for her flared even brighter. "You like a bad girl between your legs, don't you?"

"Yes," Karen whispered back, shuddering in equal parts anticipation and horror at herself.

"You and your good suburban Mommy life." Veronica tore her blouse open, deliberately popping off the buttons. "The charitable little witch, taking care of everybody else before herself. Doesn't that get old?"

"Yes."

Veronica slipped a sharp talon beneath the waist of Karen's skirt and underwear and tore the fabric apart as though it were tissue paper. "Don't you sometimes wish somebody would come along and use you like a whore?"

"Yes." Karen's knees felt like they were turning to jelly. Her old girlfriend certainly hadn't forgotten the games they used to play.

Veronica grabbed the front of Karen's bra and rent the fabric in half, tossing the useless cups and straps into the corner. And then she roughly turned Karen around, bent her over the back of the reading couch, and delivered six stinging slaps to her bared ass. The witch gasped, feeling her vulva ache sharply for Veronica's touch.

"What's that I see on your other shelf?" Veronica said, and stepped away. A moment later, she was back, waggling the 10-

inch stylized dragon ivory olisbos that Karen usually explained away as a piece of decorative statuary. "You kept your birthday present from all those years ago! I'm touched."

She pressed the tip of the chilly olisbos against Karen's swollen cleft and slowly slipped it into her, spreading her flesh wide. Karen gasped, gripping the chenille couch cushions.

"You left the door open, just a crack." Veronica leaned over Karen's perspiring back and whispered in her ear. "There's a boy out there. He has the *cutest* little wand. He's watching you. He's watching me fuck you. Do you want me to stop, Karen?"

The witch's heart pounded, and she felt a mortified blush spread over her face and breasts. She'd never, ever want Jimmy to see something like this. Why didn't he stay downstairs like she told him to, dammit? He was still too young, and all this was so wrong, and—

"No, don't stop," she replied hoarsely.

Veronica was twisting and thrusting the ivory just so against her most sensitive inner places. "Do you want me to fuck you harder?"

"Yes," Karen whispered.

"Louder," Veronica whispered back. "Say it loud so the boy can hear."

"Fuck me harder!"

The demoness went to work with a vengeance, pounding the rod into her as she reached around and began to play with Karen's clit, stroking it, teasing it, pulling it. She seemed to know exactly when Karen was about to come, and she'd back off just so, and Karen was left skating just on the brink of ecstasy for what felt like an eternity—

"Please let me come," Karen begged. "Please make me come."

"Oh, I remember what makes you come," Veronica replied,

her voice silky. "You've got this rod all juicy now—do you want it in your ass?"

Karen nodded.

"Say it!"

"Fuck me in the ass!"

Veronica pulled the now-hot olisbos from her pussy and pushed it against her tightness, drove the slippery rod home as Karen felt her squeeze her clit, and the twin sensations sent Karen rocketing over the edge. She was coming harder than she had in thirty years, arching her back to get more hard inches inside her, wailing into the pillows.

When Karen's last shudders finally passed, Veronica pulled the olisbos out of Karen and tossed it aside on the pile of shredded clothing. She spread her vulture wings over Karen, flapped once, shedding a few restless feathers, and plucked a throw pillow from the couch.

"My turn now." Veronica lay down on the floor—wings and legs splayed, her hips positioned so that anyone watching from the hallway had a clear view of her genitalia—and tucked the pillow behind her head.

Still dazed, Karen lifted herself from the couch and knelt between Veronica's muscular thighs. The demoness was staring at her with a look that Karen couldn't quite read.

"I don't expect I'll ever have this again," Veronica said softly.

"Then I'll do my best to make this worthwhile," Karen replied.

Veronica's sex had a ranker, more animal flavor than Karen remembered, but all the old familiar places still responded to her touch. The demoness writhed and moaned as Karen circled her clit with her tongue and slipped one, two, then three fingers inside her vagina. She could feel the tension rising tighter and tighter—

"Ah!" Veronica threw her head back in frustration. "I need more! More inside me."

The demoness pointed at the staff that lay a few feet away, forgotten on the floor. "That. Give me that."

Karen blinked, horrified. "That'll kill you!"

"Then kill me!" the demoness roared.

Karen had no doubt that the mere touch of the staff would burn Veronica horribly. And to drive it deeply inside her...oh no. She couldn't even begin to imagine how awful that would be.

And yet, she reached out for the staff, and with steady hands she thrust it deep into the demoness' swollen, juice-slick flesh—

—there was a flash, and the smell of brimstone and burning meat—

—Veronica was screaming, thrashing, but Karen kept her pinioned there, thinking *This will be over soon*—

—"I love you," Karen heard herself say.

—the demoness' skin was glowing, peeling away from the sizzling flesh beneath—

—and then Veronica's body exploded. The staff flew out of Karen's hands, and the shockwave knocked her flat on the floor.

It took a moment for the room to stop spinning and for her vision to clear. Karen sat up, bracing herself to see bits of the demoness blown all over the room...but instead she saw Veronica curled fetally in a nest of charred vulture feathers and cast-off pallid skin. The *real* Veronica Karen remembered, not the demonized version of her: olive skin, wine-colored lips, long, curly black hair. The girl she'd always loved had been there all along.

If she was still alive, of course.

"Veronica!" Karen crawled over to her and cradled her to her breast, trying to see if she was breathing, trying to feel for a pulse in her neck. "Are you okay? Please tell me you're okay."

Veronica slowly opened her dark eyes and stared up at Karen. "Whoa. That was intense. I'm gonna be really sore tomorrow."

"What can I do?" Karen asked. "Tell me."

"You...you got any pizza?"

"Jimmy!" Karen called.

Two beats later, the door slowly creaked open. Jimmy stood there, white-faced, looking like he was experiencing some kind of mortal shock. The front of his jeans bore an impressive dark, shiny stain. "Y-yes, Mother Karen?"

"Go call Donatos and have them deliver four large pepperonis. And put on some clean pants before the deliveryman gets here, please."

Late that night, after showers and fresh clothes and pizza, Veronica stood on the front porch with Mother Karen.

"Thank you for this." Veronica touched her bare neck. She didn't have so much as a scar to mark her as Aži Dahāka's thrall any more. "I need to try to find the missing piece of my soul, but I'll be back."

Karen smiled. "You promise?"

Veronica nodded. "This place...feels like home. I want to be where you are. If that's okay."

"Yes. Yes it is." Karen gave her a hug. "Go get whole. Be safe."

After the witch watched Veronica get into the taxi and drive off into the night, she went back up the steps to the house and went into the brightly-lit kitchen.

Jimmy was standing there, staring fixedly at his sneakers. He hadn't been able to make eye contact with her since she'd been in the study with Veronica.

"I was worried about you!" he blurted out. "That's why I came upstairs. I was worried. And then...then..."

He trailed off, blushing deeply.

"I appreciate that," she said gently. "But the next time I tell you to stay down in the basement with the little kids?"

"I'm staying down in the basement with the little kids." He nodded his head vigorously. "Yep. That's where I'll be staying."

"Good boy." She tousled his hair, then glanced over at the forgotten herbs on the cutting board. "So, let's get back to that poultice I was showing you..."

Biscuit

by Kaysee Renee Robichaud and Lucy A. Snyder

AFTER SHE PUT the _good girls don't, and when they do they certainly don't like it_ notion into the shallow and unmarked grave it deserved, the sweat-gleaming girl called Alice leaned over and brushed her blue-painted fingernails across Kai's temples and dreadlocks and stared into his eyes for a longing moment before asking, "Don't you wonder how this all happened? I mean, everything that built to this moment? All the things that had to fall in place for us to be together, right now?"

Kai nodded, his chest rising and falling with the exhausted, sex-scented breaths of afterglow. In the past two months, he'd met the kinds of people he figured only existed in pulp fiction novels. Witches. Wizards. Gangsters. But all those improbable intruders in his life seemed mundane compared to the lovely girl he held in his arms.

He could break the recent past down like it was some kind of math problem. Edict A led to Plan B which led to Events C and D...which all led to him making love to Alice. It was the future he couldn't figure out. Kai's family had taken pains to teach him that happiness never came without a cost, and when it finally showed up, happiness never stuck around long.

Right then, in Alice's dreamy embrace, he wondered if they were all wrong about that.

Five days earlier, his big brother had been trying to reinforce that lesson all over again. Kai shifted in the leather upholstered chair in Gallagher's office. As expensive as it was, he would have thought the seat should hold at least one comfortable spot. Scooting his ass around for the last five minutes had netted him zero success. Of course, his brother cared nothing about comfort. His office radiated corporate power, not humanity. There was but a single display of interesting art in the whole room: a hermetically sealed case in the corner held a set of five antique Matryoshka dolls beneath enough lamplight to reveal the certificate of authenticity but not enough to illuminate their glorious color or craftsmanship. The room's affectations were the sort aspirant Skulls cultivated to overshadow their failure to ever gain access to the Ivy League secret society.

"Let me bottom line this, Kevin," Gallagher said, oblivious to Kai's wince, "Daddy is no longer capable of supporting the flagrant waste that constitutes your current lifestyle."

Kai felt heat rise in his cheeks. "Is that so?"

"Yes, Kevin."

"Kai, Gally. People call me Kai."

Gallagher rolled his eyes. "Dialogue with me for a moment, 'Kai'. The topic: What is your ambition?"

"What is my what?" He leaned forward, resting his hands on the Gallagher's shiny desk.

"Your ambition, 'Kai'. What is it you want to do with your life?" Gallagher licked his thin lips "What do you want?"

I want Jessie, Kai thought, sitting back in the uncomfortable chair. He wanted her in every atom in every cell in his body. Jessie Shimmer had appeared; Jessie had gone. A month had passed, and she remained fixed and fresh in Kai's mind and heart and...and his soul, he supposed. She fit into all the best places in him in a way he could not verbalize. And although they had never so much as kissed, her impression remained long after she had said goodbye, haunting him more strongly than any ghost had ever haunted a house.

He told their new housemate Halulu about Jessie when he was showing the Hawaiian native her vacated room. Halulu proclaimed "She sounds like a real biscuit, man." Kai had shaken his head, no-no, trying to find a way to explain how she had been more than just another biscuit. Halulu had not grokked what he stumbled around saying, and even though Kai had since found some words to convey his feeling's depths, he doubted Gallagher would understand, either. Jessie was a rainbow bridge above coolness. She was a fire-wielding, smoking hot ganja goddess. In short, she was a *magical* biscuit.

And after she was gone, he realized she had taken a piece of him with her, too.

Tired of waiting, Kai's brother answered his own question: "It seems to Daddy and I that you have no greater ambition than to transform into an aquatic life form."

"What's that supposed to mean?"

"You've become a sponge," Gallagher said. He leaned forward, tugged a Kleenex from its box and wiped Kai's fingerprints off his expensive desk. "It's time to let you suck the lifeblood out of someone else. So, Daddy has decided—"

Kai snorted bleakly. "Oh, *Dad* decided, huh? Dad in his new lung box? With no input from you at all, huh Gally?"

"Daddy and I have decided to staunch the hemorrhaging. We both agree effective schooling is vital, so we will continue to pay for courses, providing they aren't fluff, and provided your grades in them are satisfactory. You need guidance, Kevin."

"Kai."

"*Kevin.* We will also forward you information about a better school. Something...further east."

"So I can sweat it out in a one-bedroom apartment in

Baaahston? And be just like you?" Despite his bravado, his heart beat faster at the sudden fear that he'd be forced to move and never have a chance to see Jessie again.

"Very funny, Kevin. Living in Boston could teach you a thing or two about humility and character."

"Whatever."

"You need to understand the importance of a hard day's work. Not sitting around that firetrap squat with your slacker friends sucking hookah blunts."

"Sucking what?" Kai almost laughed.

Gallagher waved his hand dismissively. "Whatever those loafers call it."

Loafer. The greatest sin in his family. Mom had been a loafer, and Dad had made her go. "What are you saying?"

"We're done throwing our good money after bad. Your allowance ends with the month. If you want rent, if you want to eat, if you want to continue funding the questionably legal 'activities' you loafers involve yourselves in . . ." He trailed off, communicating volumes with his stern glare.

"Don't stop now, Gally." Kai was amazed he could keep his voice steady, despite his stomach somersaulting and his ears burning and his eyes watering. "Hit me with the punch line." In his lap, he squeezed his hands together, praying without prayer.

"You'll need to man up, Kevin. Make your own way. Get a job or find someone else to play patron for your pathetic existence."

"Are we done?"

"Yes, Kevin. We're finished."

Kai shoved the chair's arms to rise. Though his knees trembled, and his legs felt about as strong as dead sunflower stalks, he remained steady.

Gallagher leaned back in his seat, braced for outrage or

weeping, and every second this did not happen added to his screw-faced consternation.

Kai could not manage even a ghost of a smile, but he raised two fingers in a salute and said, "Thanks for everything, Gally. Don't expect a Christmas card."

He stumbled out of the office. Doors clapped behind him, loud as cathedral bells.

He could not imagine it at the time, but later Kai would want to thank his brother for being a heartless, sanctimonious douche bag. Had Gally been otherwise, then everything that followed three days later would never have happened.

"It'll be an easy score." Halulu's grin was infectious as influenza. It almost convinced Kai the proposal was nothing more strenuous or legally questionable than selling ice-cold lemonade on a baking hot summer afternoon.

The Hawaiian pointed at Patrick: "You hold the case, and when I tell you to, you make the exchange."

Then he looked at Mikey. "You make sure the gun is in sight at all times, so no one gets any ideas. Don't stick it in your pants, unless you want to blow your dick off."

Kai asked, "What about me?"

Halulu's steely gaze rested on him for almost three full heartbeats, weighty and charged with meaning. Then he clapped him on the shoulder. "Kai, you have the most important part of all. You stay outside and keep the engine running."

"That doesn't sound important," Mikey said. "I mean, I'm the one with the gat, right?" He pointed a finger like a pistol, hand cocked ninety degrees like a total gangsta. "Woof-woof, mothafucka! The Dogz're in the hee-ouse, here to pound you asses! Cough up the cash bitches!" His finger-gun dropped. "Hell of a lot more impressive than sitting on the dock of the bay watching the tide roll away..."

"Ignore the hater," Halulu said. "You are our escape clause, Kai. Remember: There's no us without you."

"You sure this deal is hitch free?" Kai asked.

"Hell yeah," Halulu said. "I know these guys. What can possibly go wrong?"

The question brought a shiver, but Kai suppressed it. Driving was his life, now. Jessie had needed him to drive, and he found he enjoyed doing it. Worse came to worst, maybe he could make rent driving a cab or something.

Two hours later, Kai's beat-to-hell Pontiac sat across the street from the hand-off site. On the radio, fading Gorillaz beats eased the tension in Kai's head before station identification. College radio was the best; they played the uncensored shit.

Kai did not like looking at the place Halulu had led them to. It was just another Karl Road tract house, but some intangible quality cast it in a sinister light. Like the surrounding places, its blinds were drawn, and backlit by television glows or orange-yellow lamplight, but while the other houses seemed sleepily inert, this one had a jittery, predatory vibe.

Kai patted the breast pocket of his bowling shirt. The feel of the spliff reassured him. He considered lighting up. Maybe a drag would kick the shake from his hands and heart. After three seconds weighing, he muttered, "No way, man." It could wait until they were done and gone. Knowing it was there was enough. For now.

A man's gravelly voice emerged from the radio, talking about things "Everybody Knows," when the night's action veered an unexpected direction.

First, came the roar of an approaching engine. With a rubber-ripping tire screech, a Cadillac rounded the corner—a Series 61 model, a touring luxury car that must've been cherry off the line but had aged about as well as Charles Bukowski.

It accelerated down the blacktop, headlights laying the street bare. Tire rubber ground wind-tossed garbage into mash without pause. The car slammed to a halt just two houses down from Kai's Pontiac. The windshield reflected the moon, making the bone sliver crescent a lopsided grin. The passenger door swung open with a screech, and then a bundle tumbled out. Shoved or kicked. As soon as it hit pavement, the car's engine growled anew and the car leapt away. When the Caddy rolled past, Kai caught sight of a sallow-eyed man in a porkpie hat. He grinned at Kai, and his capped teeth gleamed like rusty razors.

The bundle lay still for three seconds and then sat up. It was a human being—a girl with a round face and slender throat. Wearing goth finery—though all he could make out was black crinoline, black and white checkerboard pattern leggings and plenty of leather, buckles and lacing on her top and boots. She was a pale little thing, made all the more ghostly by the moonlight. He found himself wanting to run his fingers down the graceful curve of her bare neck, feel the texture of her crinkled skirts.

She pushed herself up to sit, but even that proved too difficult. She collapsed again.

She needs help. However, Halulu's "Stay in the car" instructions echoed in Kai's thoughts, shoving away the Samaritan impulse. Then, he wondered, *What Would Jessie Shimmer Do?* That settled everything. If he didn't go, Jessie wouldn't be angry at him, probably, but she would definitely be disappointed. And that was worse than anger any day of the week.

He shoved the door open. The night's chill slapped him with fresh shivers. With each stride down the street, he muttered "This is stupid" to himself.

The dumped girl was tiny, perhaps two inches over five feet. He couldn't see any blood or obvious injuries. Makeup and night hid the finer details of the girl's features, but Kai suspected she was around his own age. Maybe nineteen? Dark hair, and dark smudges around her eyes lent her the creepy presence of a Japanese ghost. Like that girl in *The Ring*. This ghost, however, had been crying. He wanted to reach for her, but feared his touch might shatter her.

When she stopped looking through him and saw who stood over her, the girl's mouth spread wide in cartoonish glee.

"You live around here?" he asked.

She gave him nothing but a torrent of inebriated giggles. Drunk girls. He sighed; they could be so fucking annoying. And yet she was no less alluring to him than before.

"Can I help you? Get you to a porch or something?" he said.

She offered him dreamy-pleased eyes accompanied by a Cheshire cat grin.

He asked, "Want to tell me what's so funny?"

"The purple starfish," she said, "on your head. It's all wiggly."

He actually reached up before the power of silliness compelled him to blush and drop his hand to his side.

"Look," he said, stooping down to offer a hand. "Do you—?"

A firecracker pop stopped his words. He looked back toward the house as the front door jerked open. Halulu and company spilled onto the porch. No briefcase, no satchel. No baggage of any kind. They were running for the car. Patrick still had Halulu's 9mm, but it could have been a crooked baton for all the good it did him. Shadows approached the yawning doorway: gangbangers with pistols and sawed-off shotguns.

"Sweet Jesus," Kai whimpered. Before he could race back to the car, the girl caught his hand and pulled him down for a French kiss. This was clearly not the time, and yet he could not stop her or himself. His cock snapped straight before she released him. Then, she waved toward the house as though warding off gnats. At her gesture came a new commotion—the rapid fire crunches of half a dozen stones ground to gravel under a Bulldozer's treads. Still, no gunshots.

The girl said "I didn't think you'd mind if I borrowed a little. To help your guys."

From the car came Patrick's surprised "The *fuck?*" as well as Halulu's "Kai! Get your ass over here!"

No one stood in the house's doorway. The front portal was even now swinging slowly closed. Normalcy had switch to nightmarish in a single kiss' span.

"You're 'Kai'?" asked the girl. "That's a neat name."

"I gotta—"

"Take me?" she asked. From her expression, the entendre was no accident. After a languorous and agonizing moment, she added, "With you, I mean?"

"I—"

"Damn it, Kai!" Halulu was far less fun to listen to. "Forget the biscuit and do your job!"

Kai helped her to her feet, and then they hustled away together.

At the car, Halulu said, "The fuck, man?"

It was Patrick who said, "Kai found another stray."

Mikey was too busy rubbing his temple with fingertips and gun barrel to say anything.

Kai helped her into the back seat, and then slipped into the front. Though the engine was running, he turned the key again, got a grinding sound, felt a flush, and then floored it away from the house, leaving things quiet as a graveyard on December 24th.

When a red light stopped them three blocks away, the girl leaned around his headrest, so her lips were next to Kai's ear.

"I'm Alice," she said, "and I hope you'll share my Wonderland." Then, she put her palm flat on his crown and added, "Starfish," before slipping back into her seat.

The light had been green for almost five seconds before Kai remembered to accelerate.

Two hours later, they assembled in the living room so King Halulu could hold court. He took the Barcalounger and everyone else sat on the floor. "They have all the money, the meth, and what've I got? A bunch of pantywaists who can't do their fucking jobs. And a fucking biscuit."

Alice's face screwed up in confusion. "Biscuit?"

Patrick said, "He means you, honey."

"Oh." Sobriety was mostly upon her. The way she kept rubbing her forehead, Kai assumed she was enduring a hella bad hangover.

"Meth?" Kai asked, throat suddenly very dry. "I thought it was weed."

"Who the fuck wants to buy weed?" Halulu asked. "I got this from Detroit. Now we owe them big, big coin we don't have." Then, he directed a pointed glare at Mikey. "And what the hell you doing? Capping Cruz puts us in deep, deep, deep shit, man."

"The gun just went off, okay? I didn't even have my finger on the trigger." The 9mm in question lay on the floor before him, barrel pointing toward a wall.

"Guns don't fucking go off on their own. You were fucking around." Now his glare shifted to Alice. "You want to tell me what happened to those guys? How'd they go flying into the house like that?"

"What happened?" Kai asked.

Patrick played blank-filler. "We tried to make the deal. They gave us shit, and the Lone Ranger there showed his piece."

"I just wanted to scare them," Mikey said. "The gun went... it went off. And that little guy—"

"Cruz," Halulu said. "His name was Cruz."

"Cruz. He dropped, holding his side. Then, shit got real," Patrick finished. "They were set to cap us. We ran, and they got to the door, but then, they just flew backward. Like God herself swatted them out of the way." He indicated Alice with a tilt of the chin. "You have a knack for scoring special chicks, don't you?"

"Is he calling me retarded?" Alice asked.

"No," Kai said, "He's calling you a..." *What had Jessie called herself?* "A Talent."

"You guys know about Talents?"

"He brings them home regularly, now," Patrick said with a playful elbow jab. "First, the ganja goddess, now the human flyswatter. What next? An H-bomb blonde?"

"Hey biscuit. Look at me. Now, tell me. How did you do that?"

"I did a magic spell." She enunciated each syllable for extra bitchslap.

"I'm not playing with you."

"Haven't you ever heard witches are subtle and quick to anger?"

"Ain't nothing subtle about you," Halulu said, his eyes roaming her disheveled loveliness. Then he caught something in Kai's expression he didn't like. "What up, Kai? You look like someone shoved worms in your face."

"Dude, don't be such an ass to her," Kai said.

"I'm fucking pissed, here. What are we going to do?" Halulu studied his palms, then slowly curled his fingers into fists. "Witchy-tits there should be doing *something*, since this is all her fault."

"All her what?"

"You heard me, Kai."

Alice's eyes narrowed to slits. "What did you call me?"

"Bitch, please. You gonna swat me aside, now? Doesn't change the fact you're responsible. You show up and things go into the crapper. Kai forgets his fucking place. And...the gun goes off all mysterious? Sounds like voodoo bullshit to me, and you're the only one here supposedly does voodoo *bullshit*."

"Clap your hole, Halulu," Mikey said, finally looking up from the pistol on the floor. "I...uhm...misspoke around a witch once before. Trust me, you don't want one to think you're a douche bag or...or a dick. You really, really don't."

Mikey tugged his shirt as though feeling suffocated. This unconscious habit had developed in the weeks since Jessie Shimmer's spell had altered his appearance. The enchantment was not supposed to have affected him at all, but when he accidentally saw the reflection of himself transformed into a massive, sweaty, uncircumcised cock, he had nevertheless changed his tune.

"Take me somewhere we can talk," Alice said, catching Kai's hand.

"We're not done here, biscuit," Halulu scowled at her.

"Let her go," Mikey urged. "When they want to go, just let them."

With a heavy exhalation, King Halulu dismissed Alice and Kai with a courtly backhand. "You other motherfuckers got some explaining to do later," Halulu said.

As Kai led Alice to his bedroom, he heard Patrick stage-whisper, "Just enjoy living in ignorance."

Kai started apologizing even before he opened the door to his bedroom. Alice stopped his lips with a well-placed finger. "Shush, Starfish," she said.

"Are you talking to me or..." Kai licked his lips. "Or are you talking to a real starfish?"

"The purple starfish won't listen to me," she said, "but I think I like calling you Starfish. I mean, Kai is great, but everyone needs a secret name, don't you think?"

"Sure," he said. "I mean, yeah. Secret names. Like, uhm, Talent names? I don't mean to pry, I mean, I just want to—"

Her finger brushed across his lips again. "Let's go inside," she said, "and you can ask me any three things. And I'll ask you three things. And then . . ."

"And then?"

She shrugged. "And then we'll see."

She paid little mind to the cluttered floor, the spliff remnants and ashes heaped in the ashtray, the hookah collection and the smatter of CDs and comics and dirty clothes. He cleared a place on the floor, while she performed the complex task of taking off her knee high Doc Martens, and then they sat across from each other, legs crossed and knees touching. She took his hands, laid them palms up on her thighs, and tickled his love lines with her nails.

"You first," she said. "And then I'll ask one. We'll swap back and forth three times."

"What's the story with the guy who dumped you on the street."

"That was Daddy Dedman. That's what I call him, anyway. Auntie always said I should never ride with Loas, but who'd have thought she'd know?" She chuckled. "So Daddy Dedman and I had been in contact, for a while. He wanted to show me something tonight, so I accepted the ride. Turns out Daddy-D is a righteous dick. I got magic-minded before I met up with him, and maybe that was a bad idea. I might've said a little something I shouldn't have about his parentage, so he dumped me. Didn't even show me what he said he would. Wanted hitchhiker's currency for a glimpse of sweet, sweet power."

At Kai's confusion, she explained, "Ass, cash or grass. No one flies for free."

"There is so much about what you just said that I just don't understand."

"But that answers your question, I'd say."

"I guess," he said. "But it doesn't tell me anything."

"Duh. Witch." She waved as though answering roll call, then the Cheshire cat grin emerged again. "You're not a Council player, so I can be a bit more specific if you like."

"Maybe I'm happier not knowing the details?" He added, "That's totally not a question."

"It's my turn, anyway. How did you learn about Talents?"

"Jessie showed up. She needed a place to crash, rented the attic room, and she...did stuff."

"So I gathered from that Mikey guy. She left quite an impression."

"Yeah," he said. "That she did."

"Clarification: did you do it with her?"

"I wanted to," Kai said, "but she couldn't show me. She didn't have time."

"Oh really?" Alice glanced into Kai's lap with new appreciation. "I could tell you had a little bit of energy to you, but I never suspected you were an up all night kind of guy—"

He frowned. "Wait, we're talking about doing magic, right?"

"If that's what you want to call it." She cocked her head. "No, silly, I meant didja *do it*. You know, sex."

"Uhm. No. We didn't do that either."

"Ah." Alice said, and her mouth quirked in an uncertain frown. "Well, if this Jessie person's supposed to be back sometime soon, I can split. I don't infringe on marked territory."

"She's gone," he said, feeling sorrow swell in his chest. "Not coming back, I guess."

"Oh, that's okay then."

"Good." Kai nodded mechanically. Then he realized he didn't know what he was agreeing with. "Wait, what are you talking about?"

"Is that your question?"

"Nah. Sure. No. Oh, what the hell."

"You're cute, Kai Starfish." Alice's attention shifted to the top of Kai's head, and then she said, "Wait. Jessie as in Jessie Shimmer? Cooper Marron's protégé?"

"I guess?"

"You actually met that crazy babbler?"

"She talked okay when I met her. She was kind of messed up physically, but—"

"Ubiquimancers," Alice explained. "They do crazy shit. And Cooper's the worst of them. They blew up the downtown together."

"They blew up...whoa." After a moment's consideration, Kai asked, "What kind of magic do you practice?"

"Oooh, nice question." She ran her nails from his palms to his wrists. Lovely sensation and lovelier pressure. "Auntie says we're an esoteric offshoot of the OTO. The Ordo Templi Orientis? It's all a riff on Crowley's stuff. 'Do what thou wilt' with a splash of Eastern mysticism and whatevs. I call us Passion Weavers because that's how it all works in my head. It's all about energy redirection."

"What kind of energy? Like flinging fireballs?"

"Weeell, maybe. But that's totally not my forte. See, when I do this?" She ran those nails up his arms. Across his shirt, across his nipples and then higher. She leaned in until their lips met, and then another kiss triggered sensation overload in Kai's head and heart.

My God, he thought, *she's so hot.*

"When I do that," she said, "it makes energy. A little bit of ecstatic charge." She giggled. "And if I can get enough of it, I can weave an enchantment or a manifestation."

"You kiss people to make magic?"

"I have to find passion to weave," she said. "Drinking or smoking. Turning on. Kissing and full on *doing it*. Hell, singing and dancing can make a little bit. And I can borrow it from other people, too."

"How would you return something like that?"

"Well...maybe borrow is the wrong word. Does that answer your question?"

Kai had to think about what his original question had been—not easy to do, when she was drawing fiery impressions along his arms—but then he nodded.

"Why are you dealing meth with this Halulu person?"

"He's sort of new around here. He needed a room, and he paid for the attic space, which had been empty since Jessie left. No one wanted to go up there...it was spooky. Maybe haunted. At least Mikey thought so. Halulu came in, and he had some cash, not a lot. But he had connections, right? We could score poppers or..."

"Or harder stuff," she said.

Kai nodded. "Well, my allowance has been the real support for us keeping this house. I mean we all chip in, but I've had to cover a bunch of times. Jobs suck, you know?"

"I know."

"And well..." He considered the meeting with Gallagher, how to encapsulate it in as few words as possible. He managed to do it in three sentences, twenty-five words total. Then he summed up Halulu's plan as, "It seemed like a good idea at the time. Too bad Hal didn't tell us everything."

Alice remained attentive while continuing to tease him with

her nails. "Halulu is a jerk, but your brother sounds like a royal dick," she said.

"You didn't just turn him into one, did you?"

She giggled. "No, silly." Then, she added a serious, "Do you want me to?"

"No," he said, and then reconsidered, "Weeell..."

She offered a throaty chuckle. "It's your question."

"May I touch you?" He had not realized he was going to ask that until it had already made its way out his mouth.

"Ooh," she said. "Nice question."

Alice sat up straight. Her buckled leather top was not a corset proper, as it lacked boning; it blended corset with blouse, revealing her bosom in pain-free ways. She said, "Touch me, Kai." His hands turned. Palms ran along the fabric leggings and the muscular legs underneath. Breath hitched in his chest. He eased his hands past her knees, across her thighs. Not brutish, he tried for delicate pressure. Her deepening breaths suggested he was succeeding.

Nervous heat filled his head as though poured from some divine decanter and then trickled into his body. His heart pounded faster, expectant and eager, when his trembling hands eased up along the leather top. The material was lambskin soft to the touch, and the flesh beneath excited him. She bit her lower lip, when his fingers passed over the rise of her breasts. Through the layer, he discerned two solid spots. He paused to turn his thumbs around her erect nipples. She gasped and then a lusty grin spread across her face.

Alice leaned in, pushing him back as she crawled onto his lap. Kai's spine slammed the bed frame, but he did not care. She was suddenly filling his arms, and her touches ignited raw passion.

"I want you," she whispered. Her hands pulled his shirt up over his head. Heat flowed into his thighs, ignoring the denim. The smell of her perfume stung his nostrils. His cock hardened, straining against his jeans. Her waist drew figure eights, rubbing the panties against his bulge. "Why hello, Kai."

He tugged at the laces on her top. Fumbled at the buckles. Despite his fumbles, the fabric parted, baring more skin. The softness of her breasts. The tan areoles. The pert nipples. He brought the right nipple to his mouth, kissed and suckled. The left he pinched between thumb, pointer and ring fingers, a triumvirate of pressure-pleasure. She cooed, and held him to her breast with one hand. Dragged her other hand's nails along his delicate flank.

"Less teeth," she whispered. Tongue served as replacement for his lower incisors.

As his suckling and pinching intensified, her pelvis moved in faster, hungrier circles. His groin throbbed, eager to be free of this denim prison and inside her. But her breasts would not be denied. He could not pull himself away from them, except to change sides. His lips and tongue found the left nipple and her pleasure sounds drove him higher.

She leaned back, then. Drew her hands behind her to work a different sort of magic. Her top fell completely away. More flesh to explore. His mouth and hands were up to the task. Goose pimples everywhere.

She was no passive observer. Her hands and mouth explored him, as well. She caught a fistful of his dreadlocks and dragged his head back for a frantic, passionate kiss, and then she left a damp trail of kisses and licks down his throat. At the base, suction and tongue conspired, teasing him enough to render him momentarily blind. Then, her teeth found his shoulder, clamped and teased. Vision returned on a wave of colorful pleasure-pain. She worried him tender and then moved along. When she nibbled her way to his nipples, the breathing act became labor. His body was a bundle of energy and sensation and all he could voice were platitudes or pleading.

By then, they were clawing at each other's remaining clothing. She dragging his zipper down, and then pulling button open. He dragging her leggings and black lace panties down and off. When she took his freed hard-on in her hand, he reached back and dragged the bed's comforter to the floor. Her grip turned firm when she offered a couple of strokes. He moaned and she scooted back to catch his cockhead with her lips. Took him in, suckling the head. Words failed in the primal language of lust as she sucked him off. She knelt to the side, her crinoline and skirt fluffed up, baring her ass and he eased around, sliding his head between her thighs. The smell of her sex was better than any weed or single malt whisky. A moist and inviting aroma. He accepted the invitation and squeezed her ass cheeks while gobbling her sex. His tongue flitted between her clit and her pussy proper, spreading her sex as it penetrated. Her legs shivered. She fell across his chest, and they sixty-nined a while, losing kinesthesia in the blissful love fog.

She came on him with a shudder and a whimper, and he continued to eat her. She rocked back, sitting on his face. She ground against his nose and mouth, and suffocation never tasted so good. When she came again, her entire body trembled.

He urged her onto the bed. Her scent full in his nostrils and her taste full in his mouth, he clambered between her legs. Positioned himself. She caught his cock again pumped it twice and then guided the head to her pussy. He eased in, and they panted together, ecstatic sex beasts finding the primordial rhythm of a good hard screw. "Fuck me, Kai. *Hard.*" He was happy to do so.

Like everything about her, Alice's pussy was small. Tight around his shaft. Still he plunged hard and fast into her. Her hands eased under his arms. Wrapped around. Caught his shoulders. She bucked beneath him, and his cock tensed even more. The pressure was ever-building. Too high, too much.

Still he poured every ounce of energy into her. Muscles twisted along his calves, his sides, his belly. Still he pounded into her. Her moans sounded sweeter than any angel's song. When she spoke his name, it was the only motive he needed to drive harder, faster, now. *Yes*, he thought, *yes, yes, yes*.

She shivered and moaned through two more orgasms before it was all too much. "I'm going to come," Kai said, pulling back. Her nails hooked him, held him inside two heartbeats too long. His dick twitched and it spat, and there was a moment of purest intensity.

When he beheld her in that moment, she possessed an unearthly beauty. Then, heightened perceptions slipped away, and ugly realization flowed into him. "My God," he whispered, "I'm so sorry."

"Shh," she said. "You didn't do anything I didn't want."

"I came in—"

"Shh," she said. "I'm weaving." Then, she planted both palms on his chest. Like a human defibrillator, she shoved, and kicked Kai right out of his body.

First thought: *The fuck?*

Second thought: *Who is that?*

Third thought: *That's...that's me!*

Fourth thought: *It can't be.*

Yet there he was, hanging in space, over and behind himself. Kai watched his shape slump, all tension vanishing. *Holy shit*, he thought, *I died while fucking*. The idea was suddenly not as cool as it had once seemed. Then, Kai saw his body's chest fill and empty. Shallow breathing. Sleeping?

Kai tried to moan, but there was no sound. No air. No solidity. No substance.

Shit oh shit oh shit, he thought. *Worst. Dream. Ever.*

"It's no dream." Alice glanced up, away from his body and into the substanceless thing he had become. "And you're not dead. Be calm. The more you worry, the more difficult task I have to hold onto you.

What did you do to me? Damn it. He had no audible voice. He could open his spirit mouth and try to scream, but to what effect? Yet somehow she understood his words.

"I am giving you a chance to fix the foul up I've been blamed for," she said, "You can go to that place, you can interact or affect things, you can lay claim to things, and you can return. You will not have much time to decide or interact, so do not dawdle. Do you understand?"

No, he thought. Strangely enough, the panic was flowing away. This was about as real as a good hallucination. Alice's steady voice played a source of stability, of calm. It was a voice he could trust. A voice he had to trust, but more it was a voice he wanted to trust. She had fucked him into this predicament, and she alone could undo the situation's fucked-upedness, and he wanted to believe she would do just that. There was a kind of altruism to her bargain. *But really...why should I start understanding anything, now? Just tell me what I need to know.*

"See the place in as rich a detail as possible, build it in your mind and you will go there. You will have a few minutes to enter the house, to find what you want, and to mark it."

How do I mark it?

"Pass your hand through it. When you're done, come back here the same way you left. You'll come back no matter what. However, if you return under your own power instead of waiting it out you'll be less disoriented."

Why would I dick around?

"You'll get ideas," she said. "Everyone does. Maybe you've seen a little more than most, but you're free. Unbound, undetectable, unstoppable. You might become a perv like Kevin Bacon in that invisible man movie."

Do I look like Kevin Bacon?

"Right now," she said, "you don't look like much. Time is burning." She reached into her lap, brushed her fingers across her sex and shivered. Kai stared. "Go now," she said. He thought about the street. The neighborhood. That creepy house.

Then, his room turned and whirled, as though he were looking up from a toilet bowl someone had flushed. Visible space coalesced to a bright circle surrounded by impenetrable darkness, and that point slid toward him. Washed over and through him. Soaked him in inky oblivion. This emptiness had presence. It clung and then burned away like film caught in a projector gate. In that place beyond the receding darkness, he saw a nighttime street. A neighborhood. A creepy house.

Then, he was there. Wind whistled around and through him. A sprinkling of dark glitter on the asphalt marked the spot where Alice had lain. Twenty feet away he saw a drip of transmission fluid from his Pontiac.

His legs did not actually move him anywhere. He suspected the legs were a construct from his consciousness anyway. He could be formless, yet sanity needed familiarity. Maybe that gen-ed developmental psych class hadn't been a waste of time after all!

His sane human consciousness clung to shape and form, even though he was immaterial. Legs would not motivate. Thought would. A simple thought had brought him here. He willed himself to move toward the lawn, and it happened. He willed himself closer to the scary house, the scene of Mikey's crime.

The door loomed before him. The frame was cracked. The door hung poorly in it, as if it had been smashed by a SWAT team battering ram.

Before he could stop himself, he slipped through the door and part of the brick wall. The sensation was akin to passing a hand through Jell-O, though he suspected he was the Jell-O part of the equation.

The next thing he knew, he was in a living room. Battered couches clothed in red velour on the floor, amateur artwork in gilded frames on the walls. Two doorways led deeper, one toward bedrooms, the other to a kitchen and the further family room, where a television blared football and grown men groused.

He chose the quieter bedroom hallway doorway, first. The first room he poked his head into held two beds, plenty of posters and a mess of candy wrappers and CD cases. A boombox sat on the windowsill, speakers disconnected and hanging from the curtain rod like decapitated robot heads. No sign of cases. He considered inspecting the closet, but decided to check full the other bedrooms first.

The next bedroom provided pay dirt and a wake. Someone lay on the bed with arms crossed and a gray and black bandanna over his face. A wound on his side suggested his death had come from unnatural causes. At the bedside knelt another guy, dressed in the same duds, wearing a similar bandanna. This guy had broad shoulders and a neck lumpy with muscle. His hands were wide, and his fingers were thick as shotgun shells.

Overlooking everything, a three foot tall blackened bronze statue stood on a round table at the foot of the corpse's bed. The depicted figure was a feminized reaper, dressed in flowing robes that bulged over her chest, eye sockets filled with twinkling red costume jewelry. Three dozen folded dollar bills were tacked to the statue's base and robes. Kai had heard of this in his gen-ed anthropology class. Santa Muerte. Saint Death. Central Americans worshipped her despite the

Vatican's disapproval. Her rictus was too much to behold. He looked down and away as quickly as possible.

On the floor below the statue's table sat two cases. One of them was Halulu's. Still closed, still locked, still holding whatever poison he had been offering. Meth. The other case stood open, showing plenty of green packets bound in white tape. Benjamins.

This was more money than Kai had ever seen in one place. It stirred him, seeing all that money. Nowhere near the same way that Alice had stirred him, touched him, and yet...seeing it, knowing what it was, a wave of horniness flowed through him. There was no meat to arouse, no cock to engorge. It was a dull echo of the feeling. He longed to see Alice again, while his eyes once again moved up to meet the saint's terrible and terrifying face.

The idea of worshipping death had always struck Kai as pretty weird. Seeing a real statue brought a different sense to him. The thing had been carefully crafted. Each fold in the robe was the result of care and attentiveness, each crease in the skull, each tooth. Someone with real statue-making skills had gone to a lot of trouble making this, and the end result was more than weird. It was monumentally creepy, which he guessed was the point.

The weeping ganger turned, and for a cold moment, Kai feared this guy had heard his thoughts. Of course he hadn't. Still, the tear streaked face contorted with an apoplectic rage, and the eyes bore into Kai's center of spiritual mass. Then, he said, "Don't you fucking insult our saint, pendejo," and Kai knew the impossible had once more turned possible. "The fuck you doing here?"

The guy's mouth was not moving. No breath escaped his lungs.

Are you astral, too?

"Astral? I'm fucking dead, pendejo. I'm mourning myself."

Cruz. Your name is Cruz.

"That ain't my real name. They'll know the real one."

They who?

"Those who are coming for me."

Who's coming for you?

"Whoever it is that comes to take the dead to Hell. I know that's where I'm going. There's no Heaven for me. Not for all the things I've done." Cruz's eyes slit. "Are you one of them?"

Kai shook his head, and then realized that had he lied. He could have gotten away with marking the case and then vamoosing. Instead, honesty had screwed him.

"If you're not them, what the fuck you doing here, pendejo?"

Why do you keep calling me that?

"Because it's what you are. Get lost before I fuck you up."

If you hadn't noticed, we're both ghosts. I don't think either one of us could fuck up anyone.

"You don't think much, if you come where you're not supposed to be. Where you're not wanted." Now Cruz glanced toward the cases. "You're with those other guys. The *puta* who shot me. The king puta who put him up to it."

Wait. What?

"I called him a fat ass Samoan," Cruz said. "He had your boy draw down on me. So, maybe I invited the bullet I took."

I thought it was an accident.

"Accident? That little bitch had his 9 in hand. He...he..." Cruz's shade slumped. "His finger wasn't nowhere near the trigger, was it? Something else happened. Chance? Ghosts?" Terror dawned in the young man's spectral face and eyes. "How many more of you are there?"

There's only me. Even as Kai thought this, he sensed something moving behind him. It was a cold sensation, like the surprising first autumn breeze that heralded the end of another summer.

"You are so wrong," Cruz said. His attention focused on the space beyond Kai. On the door and the hallway and on the dark things filling that place. "Nino, is that you? Jesus, man, I'm so sorry, but I needed blooding. You know I had to...and who's with you?" Suddenly, the ganger turned away. "No, Nino. Don't let her come in here. Not with the stare. It hasn't dulled, has it? Hasn't changed. Death don't dull her disappointment." In a much quieter voice, Cruz said, "I'm so sorry, mamasita. I didn't mean to do it. The gasoline, it spilled. The matches were already going, and..."

Something weighty shifted in the space behind Kai. A stink like paint thinner pinched Kai's eyes shut. From the ensuing darkness, something spoke. A dozen voices, familiar but not quite right, whispered, "Turn around, Kai. We've come for you. See our faces."

No fucking thanks. He floated forward, and brushed his hand across both cases. In death's costume jewelry eyes flickered twin candle flame reflections and something else. At once, a dark mass. Like a storm cloud. But in it, moving shapes, nearly human. If he stared, he might discern them. Or might he grant them identities?

"You can't run, Kai," that droning choir said. "Not from us. Not forever. We will catch you up, sooner or later. Best it be now."

Kai squeezed his eyes shut and thought about his room, about his bed, about his body and Alice poised near it. Sweet, lovely, lonely Alice. No bending of light.

Cruz pleaded. "No, mamasita! Please don't! I'm sorry, sorry, sorry!" The last syllable raised into a shriek, before the sound of wet fabric torn and then lusty lapping.

None of it was real. It was all illusion. What could affect a being without a body? A spirit? They were eternal, weren't they?

Says who? Kai thought.

"Face me like a man, son."

Dad?

Impossible. Dad wasn't dead. He was alive. He was...he was stuck inside a steel life support tube. Because of the hate-spawned cankers and cancers and a plethora of deleterious side-effects, the old man's body had been shutting down one system at a time for months. Kai knew the story, though he could not bring himself to see the old fucker. The reason was a cocktail one part fear, one part loathing, and one part general dysfunction, shaken to a foaming fury. Besides, Dad—

"Enough running, Kai. Face what you've done, and reap what you've sown."

Dad called him Kevin, not Kai.

Leave me alone, Dad! Leave me alone the way you left mom alone! The way you drove her to...to...to do what she did! Drove her to the bottle and to the razors and to the pills and then out the door.

"I've forgiven him, Kevin." The voice had changed, now. Or a different voice had come to the fore. A woman's empathic tones. "But you? I can't forgive you, Kevin. Not for what you said. For the way you sat next to the tub and told me those terrible things when I was bleeding from the cuts in my thighs. I needed help, Kevin, and you sat there numb and crying and useless to me. It was so disappointing."

Kai turned now. *Mom?*

She was there. And Dad. And Sharon Zulkowski, who he had really liked when he was nine and she was ten and coaxed her into a game of doctor—*we were playing, and you were cool with it; you told me so!* But he had always known she wasn't cool with it. Not at all. And there was Kane Hogan, whose left eyeball Kai had cut with a carelessly thrown rock on Wilson

Woodrow Elementary School's playground—*accident! It was an accident!* Others stepped forward, when those he identified stepped back. Kai knew them all. Everyone he had ever hurt. Everyone he had ever made cry. Every person he had ever betrayed. Everyone he had stood by and let suffer, knowingly and unknowingly. They swarmed together, dark and terrible and creeping forward slow and relentless, a Hellish oil puddle.

Of course, Jessie Shimmer stood among them. She had never come back because she was caught here. Somehow this was his fault. She identified no specific crime. There was no need. Her one eye just stared with disappointment and rage, a look sharp enough to cut.

Her voice joined twenty-three other voices: "We hate you, Kai. We've always hated you, and we always will. You deserve this, our hatred. You know you do."

God help him, he did. In his mind's most remote place, the Siberia where the truth that is too terrible to acknowledge is held behind locked doors, he knew. He deserved whatever they were going to do to him. He—

He pleaded with them all, a catalog of denials, which culminated in his holy trinity. *Don't, Dad. Don't, Mom. Don't Jessie. Please don't. I didn't mean to hurt any of you. I didn't mean it. Didn't mean any of it. I'm so sorry! So sorry!*

Space shimmered. Went indistinct. Collapsed into a point. Sped toward him.

This time, it did not pass around him like water. It slapped and pulled him like a riptide. Knocked him backwards, through the table and its terrible statue.

And the cold darkness surrounded him. Cinched in noose tight. A crushing womb. Kai tried to shriek. It squeezed him into a ball. Then tighter. Smashed his spirit into its components.

As it threatened to crush him further, squeezing him to nothingness, a pinprick appeared in the womb. Through it, light. He squirted through the hole, extruded.

Into his own body.

Someone held him tight, singing nonsense in whispers. The music was damned familiar. The lullaby theme, he finally realized, from *Pan's Labyrinth*. Kai's head leaned against a bosom.

Song turned into comforting words. "It's okay, Kai. You're back. You're safe."

"Alice?"

"That's my name," she said.

"Alice, I saw my mom."

"Shhh. It's okay. You're home."

"I saw my fucking mom!"

"No you didn't," she said. That tone was firm and final.

"I—"

"You didn't see anyone you knew," she said. "And now you're back, so it doesn't matter what you saw."

But it did. Of course it did. Still, she would not tell him. Not tonight. Maybe not ever.

Some questions never got answers, no matter how much the enquiring mind needed them.

"I have to know," he said. "Tell me something, anything."

"Call it tulpa, if you like," she said. "Call it yearning. Call it a spirit vulture. Call it a feeder on the darkest guilt. Call it an opportunistic scavenger. They're different attempts to constrain an uncontainable entity. But what you saw in it wasn't real."

Her mouth found his. Taste. He realized he had been without real taste sense during his out of body experience. The feel of her reminded him that what he had taken as touch-sense was pure perception and imagination. She felt more real than anything he had encountered.

Her hair carried weight and scent and strands. Her mouth moved in a way that he could not articulate but could wholly appreciate. Her taste was heady. He wept, and their kiss broke, and she held him for a while longer.

In time, his sobbing subsided. His body relaxed. It was then he realized there were two cases on the floor. And a table with a Santa Muerte statue atop it, her costume jewelry eyes gleaming with mirth and deadly promises.

Success had come hand-in-hand with a profound emptiness.

He stood up. Pulled on his pants. Carried the drug case downstairs. Halulu still held court in the living room. Without looking up, the king said, "We need a plan for dealing with the Chicanos."

Kai dumped the case on Halulu's lap, and the Hawaiian's words—"Is this my case? No way!"—quickly trailed into confused syllables.

"This is over," Kai said. "I want you out of here before morning."

"How did you get this?" Halulu looked up. What he saw in Kai's face made him tremble. "I'll be gone, man. Gone."

Mikey still stared at the pistol on the floor. "I shot him."

"It wasn't your fault," Kai said. Mikey looked up, wanting to believe. "Halulu, take that gun with you when you go. Make it disappear."

"I will."

Kai trudged back to his room.

The act of walking was downright therapeutic. Nothing quite connected a body to life the way that walking did. It quickened the heart. Kai drew deeper breaths. Being out of his body had removed so much of his sense of what was right and real.

Alice draped the comforter over the statue. "She unnerves me."

"I can't do that again," Kai said. "Be out of my body."

Alice nodded. "I'm sorry I sprung that on you. It seemed like the only idea."

"It was a shitty thing to do," he said. She winced. "I'm sorry," he added, "but you're also right. It was the only thing to do."

"You want me to go, now?"

"Huh? Why?"

"Because I...because you...well, just because?"

He held out a hand, and she took it. He led her to the bed proper, sat with her.

"I really like you," he said. "We haven't known each other long, but it feels...feels like we should stick together. At least for a little while longer. See if anything else comes of...of whatever we've started."

"You mean that?"

He considered this for almost a second and then nodded.

They kissed, and then they loved again. Afterwards, she brushed her blue painted fingernails across his temples before she asked, "Don't you wonder how this all happened? I mean, what started hours, days, or weeks ago that built to this moment?"

Kai nodded, keeping many thoughts to himself.

"Actually, no," he finally said. "I don't wonder that at all. Wanna go to the 'Dube and get some burgers?"

She swatted his chest and laughed, and it was a pretty sound, her laughter. Kai couldn't help himself; he joined her.

Part Two:
Apocalyptic Love

Fall of Darkness

RICK DISISTO came home from the hospital, bone-tired and muscles aching from pulling bodies out of the pileup on I-70, to find his wife Lori hunched over her laptop in the bedroom, tapping away furiously. She was probably working on her virus article for the *Columbus Herald*. The airy strains of Bach's Brandenburg Concertos wafted through the house from the portable stereo, and the set of her shoulders told him that she was tense and probably not in the mood to be interrupted.

But the sight of her sitting there in nothing but her short blue silk robe, the hem riding high on those beautiful long thighs of hers...oh my. Rick felt himself getting hard. She'd put her long red hair up in a French braid, leaving exposed the lovely curve of her neck and that wonderful place behind her jaw that she loved to have kissed.

This woman *needed* to be interrupted, Rick decided, whether she realized it or not. Interrupted, carried to the bed, undressed, and made love to until they both passed out from ecstasy.

Rick stepped into the bedroom. "How's the article coming along?"

She stopped typing, sighed, stretched in her chair. "I'm up to...four thousand words."

He whistled in appreciation. She'd been having a hard time settling down to work lately; the antiviral medication they'd both been taking had been making her restless and distractible. He counted himself fortunate that he'd suffered no side effects from the drug. It was a good sign that she'd finally be able to get to work on the piece.

"You did all that today?" he asked. "I'm impressed."

"Not all. Lots, though. I think it's going to be one of my best pieces. And they'll never publish it. I have to sit there in the newsroom rewriting the vanilla 'official' crap that comes in over the wire. I can't even report on what's going on outside my own window. I have to take a sick day to get any *real* writing done...and it won't get published."

"But you can put it up on the web, right?" He kissed the back of her neck and began to massage her shoulders. Lori's muscles were knots of tension, but they slowly began to relax under his fingers. "That's why you're doing this, to get the Truth out there, right?"

"Yes, but the regular people who need to know all this don't read the kind of sites that would publish it," she sighed. "Dammit. I never thought the American press could be censored so easily."

"Most people are really scared. And the rest are vultures taking advantage of that fear," he said, remembering with sadness and anger the soldiers who'd refused to help him and the other EMTs pull the survivors from the wrecks during the day. *Unless you got some morphine for us, that ain't our job, bro.*

"First the meteors, now the diseases and looting," he said. "People are scared that the whole world is going to Hell. And when the guys in suits step in, all Big Brother-like, and say, 'We'll save you, just do as we say and you'll be fine' and out comes martial law and a soldier with an automatic on every street corner. And people just take it because at least they've still got a job and food and beer and can watch their favorite sitcom on the tube at night."

"You're sounding bitter." She pushed away from her desk and stood to face him. She touched his cheek and ran her fingers down the line of his jaw. "Something happen at work today?"

"Some truck driver went crazy and ran his rig down the wrong side of the interstate. Smashed up about 25 cars. Fifteen people died on impact, and five more died before we could get to them. We were out there for hours. A Humvee drove by, but the soldiers wouldn't help us because we wouldn't give them any drugs."

"That's terrible!"

He shrugged, then took her hands in his and kissed the backs of her fingers. "It could have been worse. They could have robbed us at gunpoint. Of course, they probably realized the traffic cops might have objected to something that blatant."

"Did the truck driver have PIPS?"

PIPS. Post-Impact Psychotic Syndrome. It had quickly come to replace AIDS as the most feared acronym in medicine. Ever since a hail of pea- to basketball-sized meteorites wrecked cities across most of the world the previous spring, people had been going crazy.

At first, the doctors thought it was simple post-traumatic stress disorder. There was plenty to be traumatized by: fires from exploded gas mains scorched Chicago and New York, basic utilities wrecked across the South and West Coast, roads destroyed, thousands killed, thousands more sickened by bad food and water and the filth of the refugee camps. And when the looters and outlaws came out of the woodwork, the feds took over and declared martial law.

But PIPS quickly proved to be far less simple than mental

stress fracturing. Victims first got a fever, then bouts of spasmodic shaking. The fever got worse, and with it came violent outbursts and paranoia. Those not prone to violence began constant nightmare word-salad babble about monsters and death.

Rick didn't know if the disease was fatal; the feds had instructed all hospitals to report PIPS cases to the Centers For Disease Control so that the afflicted could be transported to military bases for quarantine. The CDC hadn't released any official declaration of PIPS' cause, but the agency had its hands full trying to rebuild its regular laboratories while it wrestled with more mundane post-disaster illnesses like dysentery, pneumonia, and influenza.

However, Rick's cousin Gordon had worked out his own hypothesis. Gordy was an avid researcher who worked part-time as the hospital's parasitologist in addition to teaching molecular biology courses at Ohio State. He had isolated strange DNA in the blood of PIPS patients, which pretty clearly pointed to some new kind of virus. Ever since his discovery, Gordy had badgered all his friends and family members into taking antivirals as a precaution.

"We don't know if the trucker was infected or not," Rick replied. "I'm clean, though. Gordy's been a fiend about making sure our anti-infective and decontamination gear is in good working order."

He ran his tongue over the sensitive skin between her fingers, and she shivered.

"We can't have a baby while we're taking the antivirals." She pulled her hands from his gentle grip, then started to unbutton his flannel shirt.

"No. But we can still practice." He smiled and pulled her close. He could feel her hardening nipples poking through the thin silk of her robe. He felt himself go completely hard, almost painfully so. "So why don't we quit talking about all this depressing death and destruction stuff and have a little fun?"

"I haven't had a shower yet." She finished unbuttoning his shirt and planted little kisses down his sternum. "I'm dirty. I probably smell."

"I *like* the way you smell. And I'm about to get you *really* dirty," Rick said.

Lori slid her hands down his belly to the front of his jeans as she kissed him deeply. She traced the outline of his shaft with her fingertips and began to rub him. She broke off the kiss and gazed up at him, her green eyes gleaming with mischief.

"How dirty are you gonna get me?" she whispered.

"*Filthy*." He pulled an end of her belt, and her robe fell open. Rick slid his hand up her smooth pale body and cupped one of her small breasts in his hand. He leaned down and licked her nipple, sucked it. Lori moaned, and her robe slipped to the floor. Her fingers found his belt buckle and began to work at undoing the stiff leather. He ran his other hand up the inside of her thigh to tease the furry fringe of her lips.

"You're wet," he said, always a little surprised she got ready so quickly. Lori was by far the most responsive woman he'd ever been with.

"And you're wearing too many clothes," she replied, still wrestling with his buckle.

Rick helped her, and in seconds he was shrugging off his shirt and kicking his sneakers and jeans and underwear into the corner. His erection bobbed free. Lori reached for it, but he gently pushed her hand away and knelt before her. He pulled her toward him and, realizing what he wanted, she spread her legs.

Lori twined her fingers in his short brown hair and shuddered with delight as he spread her lips open with his thumbs, exposing the swollen little acorn of flesh beneath. Rick breathed on it, then flicked it with his tongue. She tasted sweet, and smelled divine.

"Oh God." Her grip tightened reflexively, her fingers clenching against his scalp.

He slid his tongue up her slick groove and moved the tip in slow circles around the opening of her vagina.

"Ohgodohgod." Lori's voice was the hoarse growl of a wild creature. She pushed his shoulders back, and Rick tumbled onto the carpet. Before he had a chance to sit up, she was on him, kissing him, straddling him, sliding his cock deep into her tight flesh.

"Oh *yeah*," he gasped. He loved it when she got rough like this.

"Make me come," she begged. "I need to come."

Rick squeezed her nipple with one hand and slid a finger between her lips to tease her most sensitive parts with the other. She was gripping his shoulders and riding him hard as if she were trying to get every last inch of him into her body.

"Oh. God." She squeezed her eyes shut. Rick felt her muscles tighten, quiver. "Oh—"

The orgasm took her, and she threw her head back and howled. Lori's muscles pumped on his shaft. Rick felt the pressure rise in his pelvis, and as his own climax slammed home like a lightning bolt he arched up beneath her. He rolled them both over and buried himself in her again and again until they both collapsed in a sweaty, gasping tangle of arms and legs.

"Oh *wow*," she said weakly. "That was great."

"We aim to please," he replied, his voice muffled by the carpet.

"Yes, and your aim was excellent. I see spots." She shifted beneath him. "Ow."

"What's wrong?" He lifted his head.

"I got rug burns on my knees."

"Rug burns? Ha! I think I'm paralyzed. I may never be able to hump again."

"Whiner. Your tongue still works. I don't see a problem."

"Hey—"

The phone rang.

"Don't get that," he said.

"Have to." She wriggled out from under him and staggered to her feet. "I'm expecting a source to call for the story."

"I'll just stay here, then," he replied, letting his face sink back into the carpet.

Another ring. He heard her pick up the phone on the bedside table.

"Hello?" Lori said. "Oh, Janine, how are you? Really? What? She did? When?" A long pause. "Oh shit. You think so? Rick and I can go up there to check things out. He doesn't know us. Could you...yes, that'd be great. We'll let you know. Okay. 'Bye."

Lori hung up. "Oh shit. Rick, we've got to go to Cyrusville tonight."

"Tonight?" He blinked. "Why? What's in Cyrusville?"

"Annie disappeared yesterday, and Janine thinks her ex-husband Harold might have kidnapped the girl or encouraged her to run away. Harold runs a bed-and-breakfast up there, and that's the logical place for him to be keeping the girl. Janine's absolutely desperate to go up there and look for her daughter, but she can't get a travel permit..."

"But *I* can, provided I'm responding to a medical situation," Rick finished. "Hm. I guess I can sweet-talk one of the ER doctors into signing for me. And I suppose calling the police about this would be a monumental waste of time...they probably have hundreds of unsolved missing persons reports on top of everything else."

Rick frowned. Annie was a pretty 16-year-old who'd lost her left hand to a meteor fragment that punched through their condominium. She hadn't coped well since the disaster, and had become by turns withdrawn and emotionally unstable. Janine and Harold had divorced when Annie was a baby, and as far as Rick knew Harold had never sought much contact with his daughter.

"Did she say why she thinks the guy kidnapped Ann?" he asked. "Seems just as likely she's run off with a boy."

"Janine said Harold's called them a lot recently. He got nutty-religious after the disaster, and now he's on this big apocalypse kick. He seems to think we're in the End Times, and Janine thinks he wants to die with his family near him. His brother died in the Chicago fires, so Ann is his only living relative."

Lori paused. "She didn't say it, but I think she's worried he might decide to speed them along on their journey to Heaven, if you catch my drift."

"Swell. So, the plan is to drive up there, pose as newlyweds, get a room for the weekend and snoop for the girl?"

"That would be the plan, yes. Janine said she'll pay for our room and gasoline."

"What about your article?"

"It'll keep 'til we get back. Finding Annie is way more important."

Rick sighed dramatically and sat up. "I suppose we're gonna have to have lots of wild monkey-sex, too."

She sat down beside him and gave him a long, slow kiss. "Lots and lots and lots," she smiled.

Their evening trip to Cyrusville took about three times as long as it should have. The queue for $8-a-gallon gas was ten cars deep at the Shell station, and once they got to the hospital it took Rick a solid 45 minutes to get his permit. Once they were on the highway, they had to pass through two different Army barricades. Lori was worried that the soldiers would search the car and confiscate the handguns and ammunition they'd brought with them for self-defense. But the permit and Rick's easy banter got them through the checkpoints cleanly.

Lori admired her husband's way with people. He could put almost anyone at ease, a talent for comfort that had served him well as an EMT. He certainly had the most amazing effect on *her*. Sometimes, just the smell of him was enough to turn her on. Even when she was stressed-out and grumpy, a look, a smile, a squeeze of his hand...and suddenly she would want to lick every square centimeter of his body.

He was one of the hottest men she'd ever laid eyes on, and in her eyes he just kept getting hotter every day. He had the kind of blue eyes that would put Paul Newman's to shame. He had a great body, too, even with the love handles he'd gotten from eating one too many times at the Chinese buffet down the block from the hospital. And he filled out his blue jeans in the most delicious way. If he were any bigger, he'd be *too* big.

Once her worries about the soldiers had passed along with the second checkpoint, her hand kept migrating across his thigh as he drove. By the time the bed-and-breakfast came into view, silhouetted by the setting sun, he was erect and visibly flushed in the glow from the dashboard lights.

"Quit that," he said as he pulled the car onto the long, wooded drive leading to the inn.

"Quit what?" she asked innocently, tracing circles on the inside of his thigh.

"*That.*" He gently pushed her hand away. "Keep your hands to yourself, little missy, or I won't be able to walk to the front door."

"Spoilsport."

The inn had begun its life as huge old farmhouse. Harold had added on new rooms and modern amenities like a swimming pool. In the dying light, Lori could see that the exterior needed a fresh coat of paint. Likely the bed-and-breakfast business had suffered considerably since the meteor disaster a year ago.

Rick parked the car in the small lot in front of the house. Lori slipped her pistol inside her handbag, and Rick put on his shoulder holster and then put his leather bomber jacket on to hide his revolver. They got their overnight bags from the back seat, locked up the car, and headed for the front door.

A chime sounded as they stepped through the front door into the anteroom. The interior was tidy, the hardwood floors shined and the table bearing the guest register dusted. A broad mahogany staircase rose up at the end of the anteroom, and a hallway opened to the right of the stairs. Even if business had been bad, Harold was apparently still trying to keep the place up.

She heard footsteps, and soon a balding, paunchy man of about fifty stepped into the anteroom from the kitchen.

"May I help you?" he asked, eyeing them uncertainly. "We're the Smiths," Rick replied. "We have a reservation?"

"Yes, of course," the man replied, relaxing a little. "Welcome to the Willow Ridge Inn. I'm Harold Wilkins, the proprietor. You wanted the first-floor Garden Room, I believe?"

"That the one with the feather bed?" Rick asked.

"That would be the one," Harold smiled. "It's the best bed in the house; I guarantee you'll get a great night's sleep. Now, if I can get you to sign the register...and I'm afraid I'll need $140 up front. In cash."

"No problem." Rick dug out his wallet and extracted a wad of twenties.

Harold accepted the cash and tucked it in his breast pocket.

"It's a terrible thing to have to take cash up front...but we've had one too many folks run out in the middle of the night. I just can't afford that sort of thing."

He took a deep breath, then gestured toward hallway. "Your room is the second on the left down that hallway. After you, please."

Harold continued talking as they ascended the stairs. "If you need to get anything else from your car, you'll need to do it in the next half hour or so; I'm about to turn on the house alarm. Can't be too careful these days."

Which was true; the looting and general increase in robberies since the disaster had been one of the major reasons the feds had implemented martial law. She imagined that an isolated inn like this one would be a prime target for thieves.

"Have you had any trouble?" she asked. "With burglars, I mean."

"No ma'am. I've barely had visitors since the martial law started," he replied.

He shook his head. "What a mess the world's become. I have to believe that the Lord's got better plans for us, that He's going to put an end to these terrible times soon. But until He decides it's time, we just have to keep going and do our best to live upright lives."

They came to the end of the hallway. "Here's your room," Harold said, pulling his keyring out of his pocket and unlocking the door. "There's a small fridge in here with pop and juice and water and some snacks; feel free to help yourselves."

Lori and Rick stepped inside and deposited their bags by the door. The room was cheerful and brightly-lit by two antique lamps. Rose-patterned paper decorated the walls. A nubbly cotton bedspread covered the four-poster oak bed, and the windows were dressed in lace curtains. An antique chest-of-drawers and a modern luggage stand sat beside a door leading into the bathroom. A small writing table with a high-backed chair completed the furnishings.

"No one else is here right now," Harold continued. "So you've got the run of the floor. I can serve you breakfast pretty much anytime you want after 7 a.m.; just dial "0" on the phone beside the table an hour or so before you're ready. If you need anything else during the night, just give me a ring. Checkout time's 4 p.m., and the second night's half off if you decide to stay another day. If you're looking for something to do tomorrow, there's a nice place to hike near the creek.

"Can I get you folks anything else?"

Rick shook his head. "Nope, I think we're good. Thanks."

"All right. You folks have a good night." He handed Rick the room key and left, shutting the door behind him.

When she was sure the innkeeper was out of earshot, Lori said, "He seems like a decent enough guy. He isn't setting off my nut-radar, anyway."

"Mmm-hmm." Rick stepped up behind her, pulling her close. She could feel his erection pressing against her. He slid his hands up under her blouse, beneath her bra. He fondled her breasts, teasing her nipples into hardness. She felt herself getting wet.

"Wait...we should look around first," she said, her protest sounding unconvincing even to her own ears.

"You've been giving me blue balls since Ovalville," he replied. "We're not going *anywhere* but that bed over there. If we make it that far."

He pressed a hand between her legs, and she moaned at the ache of desire that coursed through her. She leaned back against his hardness and rubbed her ass against him. He began to kiss her neck, and she craned her head back so he could reach her mouth. They kissed deeply, passionately. His hand found her zipper, and before she knew it he was tugging down her jeans and panties.

Lori turned in his arms and buried her face in his neck, licking his stubbly skin, nipping his earlobes. She unzipped him and slid her hand inside his boxers to find his rock-hard shaft.

"Do me, oh God, please do me *now*," she whispered hoarsely.

He helped her out of her blouse and bra, then peeled off his rugby shirt.

Lori stepped toward the bed, but he grabbed her hips and held her fast. Realizing that he wanted to fuck her from behind, she bent over and braced herself against the footboard.

She guided him with her hand, then gasped as he slid into her. God, he was so big, and she wanted every last inch of him inside her. She arched up on her tiptoes as he began to thrust in and out, kissing her back and neck, his coarse pubic hair rough against her buttocks.

He slipped a hand around her waist and slipped a finger between her lips to pleasure her. His touch on her inflamed flesh sent a ripple of fire through her loins.

"You're so tight," he gasped. "I can't get enough of you."

His fingertip ran sweet electric circles around her clitoris. It was almost too much to bear. She arched up against him, heart pounding, stretched tight on a rack of delight.

"You're going to come, aren't you?" His voice was hoarse with lust. "Come for me, baby. Come for me!"

She came with a shuddering gasp, and as her muscles pumped madly on his shaft he gave a throaty moan and she felt the twitch and spurt of his climax inside her.

Her arms gave out, and they tumbled forward onto the bed.

She rolled over onto her husband and planted wet little kisses all over his sweaty face.

"That was great," she whispered.

"Oh yeah." He looked dazed, as if he'd been hit by a truck.

"Again?" she asked hopefully.

"Maybe in a minute," he slurred. "I gotta rest for a little bit."

She pulled the bedspread down and helped him crawl under the covers. He was snoring mere seconds after his head hit the pillow.

Lori, on the other hand, was wide awake. She lay beside her husband feeling increasingly restless and sticky. Finally she got up and went into the bathroom to get cleaned up.

As she dried off with a fluffy white towel, she heard a faint noise coming from the air vent. She stopped, leaned in close, strained to hear. Sobbing. She heard faint sobbing.

Her heartbeat quickened. Could it be Annie?

Lori dressed quietly and put on a pair of soft-soled canvas sneakers. Rick mumbled and rolled over, but didn't wake up.

I'll just let him sleep, she decided. *It won't take me five minutes to look around a little.*

Lori dug her pistol out of her purse, checked the clip, and stuck it in the waistband of her jeans. She closed the door behind her and started to creep down the hallway. The house was dark; evidently the innkeeper had already turned in for the night.

As she reached the anteroom, she stopped, holding her breath to better listen. Yes, it was definitely sobbing, from... below. The basement.

Lori snuck through the kitchen. The door to the basement would probably be somewhere near the pantry. After a few minutes of hunting in the dark, she found a low wooden door, the bolt latched but not locked. The sobbing noise was louder here; it was a girl's voice.

Lori slid the latch open as quietly as she could and swung

the door open. She could see the soft yellow glow from a small lamp.

"Ann?" Lori started down the basement stairs. "Annie, is that you? It's Lori."

"L-lori?" the girl stammered. "Please don't come near me. The monsters have got me. I'm a monster. Don't come near me."

Lori got to the bottom of the stairs. The first thing she noticed was the smell: the air had a foul, coppery stink, like blood and insects.

Then she saw that the teenager was huddled under a quilt on a small bed in the corner of the basement. Harold had evidently taken some pains to make the corner look homey: a handmade rug softened the concrete floor, and there were decorative fabric hangings on the cinderblock walls. A mostly empty two-liter bottle of water and an empty plate sat on a small table beside the bed.

The teenager was shivering, her face beaded with sweat. Her eyes were glassy with fever, and her face looked bloated and skewed, as if the planes of her face had shifted. "The monsters have me, Lori."

Lori's heart fell to the bottom of her stomach. PIPS. Her cousin had PIPS. "Oh, God, Annie. Not you, too..." she whispered.

"But they gave me back my hand," the girl giggled. "Only it's not mine."

The girl pulled her left arm from beneath the quilt. The year-old scar tissue on her wrist had erupted in a hard, shiny, black-purple mass, and from it extended four long, jointed insectoid digits. The first two twitched spasmodically.

Lori let out an ear-piercing scream and jumped back.

The girl didn't seem to notice her horror. "See?" Annie giggled again. "Somewhere there's a monster who's got no hand."

Sweet Jesus. Bile rose in Lori's throat, but she forced down the fear and revulsion she felt. Her legs were telling her to run run run far away, but this was her best friend's daughter, a girl in trouble and pain and she had to help her.

Lori had never seen PIPS do anything like this before. Some sufferers had come down with strange cancers, but *this*...this was no cancer. Cancer didn't make working parts. She knew she had to get the girl to the hospital, fast.

"I'm—I'm gonna get you out of here," Lori stammered, then turned to run back up the stairs.

Harold stood in the basement doorway with a shotgun. He pointed the barrel at her and descended the stairs.

"She's not going anywhere," Harold said, his voice equal parts sadness, anger, and menace. "And neither are you. Take that gun out and drop it on the floor. Then kick it into the corner."

Lori reluctantly did as she was told. You didn't argue with a 12-gauge.

"Can I have some more water, Daddy?" the girl asked, oblivious to the gun. "I'm really thirsty."

"For Christ's sake, she needs a doctor!" Lori exclaimed. "She's your own daughter...how can you let her suffer like this?"

"It's God's will. My daughter came to me in her hour of need, and now I have to take care of her and let her transformation take its course."

"T-transformation?" Lori stammered.

"My skin hurts," the girl said. "I think it's gotten too tight. I'm really thirsty, Daddy."

"I'll get you some Gatorade in a minute, honey."

He turned his attention back to Lori. "Remember the Great Flood? The Lord saw that what he created had gone bad, so he flooded all the Earth, sparing only the pure to start anew. This time, he's realized that we humans are impossibly flawed. The meteors came from Heaven, you know. None of the scientists expected them. They're the new Flood. Most people will be killed, but He will recreate the pure into his own image.

"We humans have become so corrupt that we see ugliness as beauty and beauty as ugliness. I know that my daughter is pure, and God must have a reason for what she's going through. You've seen her hand. She's becoming one of the Lord's new children, ugly in the eyes of man but beautiful in the eyes of Heaven."

"It's a virus," Lori pleaded. "This isn't God's will any more than the Black Death was."

Harold raised the shotgun, pointing it at her face. His expression was one of profound sadness. "Where's your husband?"

"Upstairs. Asleep. What are you going to do, shoot us? *Murder* us? God doesn't let murderers into Heaven."

"This is all part of God's test of my faith. I have to protect my daughter," he said quietly. "Let's go find your husband."

He nodded toward the stairs. "After you, miss."

She walked back up the stairs with the hard barrel poking her in the back. They stepped into the kitchen.

Suddenly, Rick jumped out at Harold from behind the corner. He jerked the barrel up, and the gun discharged into the ceiling with a deafening boom. Hunks of plaster rained down. Lori dove out of the way as the two men wrestled with the weapon.

Rick tore the gun out of Harold's hand, spun and whacked him across the face with the hard wooden butt. Harold went down and didn't come back up.

Lori found the switch plate on the kitchen wall and turned on the lights. Her husband stood there gasping for breath, bare-chested, a pistol tucked in the waistband of his jeans.

Harold lay face-first on the floor, blood spilling from his mouth and nose. Rick knelt and felt for a pulse.

"Is he okay?" she asked.

"I think he's just unconscious," Rick replied. "But I might have broken his jaw."

He stood and faced her. "I heard you scream and woke up, so I came down here...Jesus, Lori, why didn't you take one of the guns?"

"I—I *did*," she stammered. "But he came up before I knew he was there."

"Well, go find some twine or duct tape. We better tie him up 'til we figure out what to do next."

Lori started rummaging through the kitchen drawers. "Annie's in the basement. She's got PIPS. But something's... something's really wrong with her..."

Rick nodded. "Okay, I'll go take a look." He padded down the stairs.

Lori found a roll of blue duct tape in the bottom kitchen drawer. She knelt beside Harold and had just finished taping his wrists together behind his back when Rick ran back up the basement stairs with her pistol in his hand.

"Oh man. Oh man." Rick's face was white, and his hand shook as he handed her the pistol. "I have *never* seen anything like that before. We've got to get her to the hospital so Gordy can examine her."

"Can he send an ambulance with an isolation unit up all this way?" she asked.

"He'll have to, won't he? He'll be at home now. I've got his number in my notebook. Let's get back to the room and I'll call him."

Once they were back in their room, Rick tossed the shotgun onto the bed and started digging through his overnight bag. Lori told him about her conversation with Harold in the basement.

"I don't think he's infected," she finished. "Though he's seriously delusional."

"I dunno...he might be onto something with the meteors. There's a relationship between the virus and the meteors that nobody's really addressed." Rick found his notebook and started sorting through the handwritten scraps of paper he'd stuck inside the front cover.

"Are you saying you buy his 'God's newest Flood' notion?" she asked.

"No. The God I know would not have done this. But this is *altering* that girl. She ran away how long ago?"

"Four days ago."

"And she wasn't visibly sick?"

Lori shook her head. "Janine would've mentioned it if she were. But I suppose if she were getting the paranoia before the fever, that would explain why she ran."

"That means she's grown something approximating a new hand in less than a week. That's an awful lot of cellular activity. No virus that could do that. So I'm thinking either it's a bioweapon that was released or escaped during the disaster and then mutated, or..." He trailed off.

"Or it came from the meteors?" she finished. "That's a heck of a stretch, Rick. Martian flu? How would it survive the extremes of temperature? How could a totally foreign genetic system interact with ours?"

"Okay, okay, it's a stretch. Forget I said anything." He ran his hands through his hair. "Let me call Gordy, and we'll get her to the hospital and see if anything can be done for her."

"Daddy? Daddy, I'm thirsty," they heard Annie call. Her voice was strangely distorted.

Harold let out a short, hoarse yell of terror, then began to pray: "Our Father who art in Heaven, Hallowed be Thy name.

No, Annie, Daddy loves you, don't—Aaah! My Lord please—noooOOOooo—"

His scream abruptly ended in a wet gurgle. Close behind it came a damp ripping noise, and a snuffling sound.

Then everything was quiet.

"Oh Jesus," Rick whispered. His face had gone white. "Oh Jesus."

The hairs on the backs of her arms were standing on end, her heart beating fast as an ancient instinctive fear rose like floodwaters inside her.

Daddy, my skin hurts. I think it's gotten too tight.

"Let's get the fuck out of here," Lori squeaked.

They shoved their belonging back into their overnight bags and raced down the hall toward the front door.

As they hurried past the kitchen, Lori glanced inside. Harold was in pieces. A raw *thing*—which at first glance looked like a gigantic black beetle wrapped in the body of someone who'd been turned completely inside-out—was crouched over Harold's remains, lapping up his blood with a long, proboscis-like tongue.

At second glance, Lori saw the clumps of blonde hair falling from the thing's head, saw the broad, multi-toothed mouth and the razorlike claws gleaming on the ends of the black, jointed legs that had erupted from raw flesh.

Lori screamed.

The thing jerked its head up. "Lori, I'm thirsty," it whined in its weirdly little-girl voice. "I'm thirsty, I'm thirsty."

The Annie-thing scrabbled toward them with alarming speed.

"Oh shitshitshit!" Rick fired the shotgun into the horror again and again.

In seconds, it was over. The Annie-thing was a sodden mass just a few yards from Harold. Dead.

Lori and Rick didn't waste time. When they pushed open the front door, the alarm sounded, loud as Apocalypse. They pelted across the front yard to their car, scrambled inside, and burned rubber back to Columbus.

Dawn was seeping into the black sky when they tumbled into their own bed. They held each other close, listening to their hearts hammering in each others' chests.

"I can get you something to help you sleep, honey," Rick offered.

Lori shook her head and kissed him softly on the cheek. "I don't think I want to sleep. Nightmares, and all that fun stuff." She rubbed her eyes. "God, how can I ever tell Janine about what happened tonight?"

"Tell her we had car trouble and didn't get up there," he suggested. "Tell her...anything. Just not what really happened."

"What *did* happen?" she wondered. "The feds take all the PIPS patients away to the quarantine bases before they get really bad...what if what happened to Annie's happening to other people?"

"A bioweapon." He shuddered. "And she did get hit by a meteor. We *know* that for a fact. She gets wounded by a meteor, she gets PIPS, and turns into a monster. There's too much here for coincidence."

She snuggled close to him, shivering. "I feel so awful about Harold and Annie. What a terrible way to die."

"We did the best we could...what else could we have done?"

"I don't know," she replied. Her expression of worry hardened into determination. "But I *do* know what I can do about it *now*."

"What?" he asked.

She rolled away from him and got out of bed. "Finish my virus article," she said. "If the local paper won't run it, I'll put it on the Web. I'll print out copies myself and tack them to every corkboard in the county. I'll stick copies in bottles and float them down the river. Whatever it takes."

Rick watched her type for a long time before he finally drifted off to sleep to the sound of her clicking keys. He had the feeling that the world was about to take an even steeper plunge into darkness, that Annie's transformation was only the beginning.

But he also knew that their love was strong, stronger than any damned virus, and in the end, that was what mattered to him most. It wouldn't be easy, but they'd find a way to survive.

No matter what.

In The Wilderness

SISTER CORDELIA kept catching herself staring with lust and dread at the little black cabinet above her sleeping pod. Each time, she'd mutter a prayer and redouble her efforts to stay busy. But after five hours of recalibrating the biosensors, compiling atmospheric data, and cleaning the *Tortoise's* air and water filters, she had little left to do. Except sleep, plug into the dull chatter on the web, or watch one of the syrupy ecodramas on the satellite feed.

Or open the cabinet.

She stared at the little black aluminum doors. The *Tortoise* was creeping through rocky scrublands. Dead wood and sandstone chunks popped beneath the heavy steel treads. The vibrations through the floor were low and strong, the thrum of the motors an insistent rhythm that went up through her legs into her belly. She realized her panties were damp.

Cordelia made herself step away from the cabinet and stared out one of the round starboard windows. Desert was slowly turning to grassland as the vehicle rolled northward, 20 kilometers per hour on its winding tour of North America. The *Tortoise* could probably triple that speed if it could run on gas or alcohol instead of solar cells. But that was forbidden in Gaia's wilderness; the vehicle's heavy footprint was insult enough to require nightly prayers. The sin of emission was unforgivable.

The sky was a perfect blue. Purple thistle, red paintbrushes and yellow asters had sprung up in the trench of an almost-dry creekbed. A riot of butterflies delicately sparred for position among the blooms. She imagined that the weedy wildflowers would smell like a divine fever, hot and rank and beautiful.

Cordelia pressed her cheek against the warm glass. She was sweating in the perfect air conditioning. She longed to be able to open the doors of the *Tortoise* and let the sun burn her face as she picked a bouquet. But that was impossible. The flowers, the butterflies, even the microbes in the soil could be harboring the polymorphic panvirus that had wiped out most of the Earth's human population over fifty years before. The virus had probably escaped from someone's bioweapons laboratory. When no consistent cure could be found, no one would admit to creating it. The plague now had the sheen of myth, and many people were convinced Gaia herself had generated it to rid herself of a nasty case of human fleas.

If Cordelia were exposed, she'd seem fine for days, maybe weeks. But then would come the cramps, and the internal hemorrhaging as her mucous membranes turned to bloody lace. Her immune system would shut down, and the bacteria in her gut would revolt and eat her from the inside out. No amount of fresh air and flowers was worth that.

Turning away from the window, she faced the cabinet. She slid the doors open and pulled down the white plush teddy bear her husband Sam had won for her at a carnival game three days before their third and final wedding anniversary. It held a little sewed-on red satin heart between its stubby forepaws.

Just a little something to remember me by when I can't be here for you, he'd told her, not realizing he'd die in a shuttle crash only three weeks later. Or that she'd spend broken, lonely years trying to recover until she finally found a small refuge from her grief by joining the Sisters of Survey order of the Temple of Gaia.

She buried her face in the fur, breathing in its faded rose-and-spice scent. The delicate odor sent a shiver down her spine to pulse as a point of heat in her vagina. The bear's black eyes gleamed at her as she impatiently flipped aside the cover on the data jack behind her left ear. She unspooled the lead from the VR unit hidden in the bear's belly and plugged in.

Suddenly, she was standing naked in the cool evening dimness of their old apartment in Philadelphia.

"Is it recording?" Sam asked, running a velvet-soft finger down her spine. She shivered with delight, her nipples hardening almost painfully.

"I think so," she said. "I can't really tell. Why do you want me to record this? I'd think you'd want one of yourself."

"I want to know what this is like for you," he replied, playfully sliding his cock against the inside of her thigh. "I'll be able to do better for you once I've had sex in your skin."

"So then you'll have to record it next time...so I can learn what it's like for you."

"If you wish. But I don't think it could teach you anything you don't already know by heart."

He gently turned her around and began to kiss her hand, licking the delicate skin between her fingers. She cupped his balls with her free hand, then slid her fingers up the corded shaft of his cock. She loved to play with it, loved the feel of it: the soft, veiny skin over the iron-hard shaft, the comfortably spongy tip. He could last all night if she needed him to.

As she stroked him, she felt her own parts swelling, moistening, opening. She could feel his pulse in his shaft. Her vagina burned to feel him inside her, but it was too soon. She wanted to savor the moment. She started nibbling his neck, breathing in his musky scent and tasting the salt on his skin. She circled the head of his cock with her thumb and forefinger and gently squeezed. He shuddered.

"Oh God, Delia...I want to fuck you so bad."

She nipped gently at his earlobe. "Not yet," she whispered.

Cordelia led him to their bed, and sat down. His cock bobbed a few inches away from her face. She slowly licked off the glistening, salty prejack beading from the tip, then tickled his frenum with her tongue. Sam groaned.

"No, this is supposed to be for *you*," he protested weakly. "Hmm, well, since you put it like *that*..."

She slid back on the bed to make room for him. He practically leapt on top of her, devouring her face with little kisses, licking her nipples, nibbling her earlobes until her body was thoroughly rashed in goosebumps. He gently parted her thighs and slid two of his fingers against her wet groove, circling, teasing at the slit of her vagina.

"Oh, Sam, go in," she moaned.

"Not yet."

He pulled her legs up over his shoulders and parted her lips with his thumbs. He exhaled hotly against her vulva, then flicked her clit with the tip of his tongue. She sucked in her breath and arched her back. He licked her again and again, each a tiny bolt of lightning.

"Please, go in," she begged breathlessly.

"Roll over," he said, pulling back.

She rolled up onto her hands and knees. Sam got up on his knees behind her and reached around to tease her clit as he entered her. His cock burned sweet as he slipped inside.

He rubbed her in time with his slow thrusts. He leaned down over her, his chest hair tickling her back, and caressed her breasts with his free hand. Cordelia arched her back and leaned into him, savoring the feel of his warm body over hers.

"Harder," she breathed. "Spank me hard."

She felt like a watch spring wound so tight it was about to shatter. She held her breath, and just when she thought she could stand no more the orgasm took her. Every nerve was afire and green sparks bloomed behind her eyes as her inner muscles clamped down on Sam, and he was coming, too, oh God it felt good...

They collapsed in a sweaty heap on the bed. She snuggled close to him, breathing in his musky after-sex smell. He held her, stroking her damp hair. She wished she could stay there in his arms forever.

The recording abruptly ended.

Cordelia found herself standing by her sleeping pod, staring down into the silent black eyes of the teddy bear. Her heart was still pounding. As the beat slowed, she was overcome by a horrible emptiness, a lonely, cancerous ache in her chest and bones. Sam was the very definition of her desire, the alpha and the omega of her dreams. And he was dead. Dead, and gone, and turned to dust, and still she pined for him.

How many times had she played the bear's recording? Five hundred? Five thousand? She could not come without it. She'd tried to masturbate, but her flesh refused to respond under her own touch.

The toy suddenly seemed as heavy as a lodestone. She knew it wasn't healthy, re-living the past. Picking at her wounds. If she had any sense, she'd throw the toy away. She'd tried, many times, but she'd get to the trash recycler and discover she could no more shove it down the chute than she could gouge out her own eyes.

Feeling defeated, she opened her sleeping pod and lay down. How long had it been since she'd seen another person? She counted backward in her mind: a year and a half. Her supplies were air-dropped every month; she had brief chats with the pilots, but that was all the human contact she'd had. In another year, the *Tortoise* would reach the domed resettlement that had sprung up over the decayed wreck of San Francisco. There were over 50,000 people there now. She had no idea how she'd be able to relate to any of them.

She curled up around the bear and cried herself to sleep.

She jerked awake as the engine alarm went off. The vehicle wasn't moving. Rubbing the sleep from her eyes, she hurried to the control console to shut off the insistent beep. She blearily scanned the readout. Something was jamming the starboard tread; probably a churned-up dead tree limb had gotten wedged in the machinery. Damned nuisance. Tread jams were rare, but when they happened, she was usually in for hours of hard, tedious labor.

Cordelia pulled Gaia's altar from the cabinet beneath her sleeping pod and set it up beside the airlock. She reverently touched the vial of seawater, the lichened rock, the dried sprig of mistletoe, the white staghorn.

"Dear Mother, please forgive the trespass I am about to commit," she prayed aloud, closing her eyes. Her voice sounded too loud, raw in her own ears; disuse had left her vocal cords rough and uncertain.

"I must enter into your lands to attend my machine so that I may fulfill our quest to understand your cycles and avoid the sins we have committed against you in the past. Should I damage your creatures or disrupt your environment, I beg forgiveness, for I intend no harm."

She touched the altar items once more, in reverse order, and snuffed out the incense sticks. She put it away, then found her toolbox and shrugged into her rubbery environment suit, work gloves and boot covers.

The sun was a dull red eye peeking over the horizon. The vehicle was stranded on the crumbled remains of a highway a few hundred yards away from a shallow arroyo. By now, the road was more shin-high grass than pavement.

The area seemed to be an ecotone between the Chihuahuan Desert and the Great Plains, though the nearby water meant that the landscape was dotted with little groves of mesquites, mountain cedars and oaks. A few rocky hills rose a mile or two to the north. This land had probably been a part of Texas, before the plague. The survivors' subsequent conversion to Gaiaism had erased the political boundaries of America's heartland. With everyone dead and the mutable virus still vectored in a host of plant and animal carriers, it seemed best to re-build in the deforested coastal sprawls and leave the rest to return to wilderness as the Earth Mother saw fit.

Cordelia shut but did not secure the airlock and waded through the thickly-dewed grass toward the troubled tread. It felt strange to walk across the grass. She hadn't been outside in an env-suit in nearly a year and a half. Her breath fogged on the inside of her clear acrylic faceplate; it was chilly out this morning. Catclaw briars snagged her env-suit, and her heart jumped in alarm. But the material held.

She reached the problem. A four-foot-long dead branch the width of her forearm was sticking out from the *top* of the vehicle, wedged at a 60-degree angle through the gap between tread and chassis into the wheels.

This was no accident.

She turned around, her breath catching in her throat. Had she heard footsteps? She strained her ears, but could hear nothing but her own heart and the eerie coos of the doves waking in the brush.

Who could have done this? No one had detected any surviving settlements out here in the half-century since the plague drove everyone to the ocean. Could it have been Reclamationist terrorists? No, they'd have used a bomb, not a stick. She'd be dead by now.

Best to get out of here as quickly as possible. She grasped the branch and pulled, digging her heels into the muddy ground. The branch came free after a few hard tugs. She tossed it aside and leaned over to shine her flashlight into the gap. It didn't look like there was any damage, just a few wood chips that would be ground to powder.

She pulled her largest screwdriver out of her toolbox and crept back to the airlock. The tool was a better weapon than nothing, but she wished she had the autopistol that was locked in a drawer beside the control console.

Both the interior and exterior airlock doors were standing wide open. A few muddy shoeprints marked the steps and the floor of the airlock. Cordelia felt her blood run cold. Was the intruder still inside?

Holding the screwdriver like a knife, she went into the airlock and peeked inside the cabin. It was empty, except for more muddy prints. None of the cabinets were big enough to hide in.

Breathing slightly easier, she pulled the outer door shut and locked it behind her. She quickly peeled off her boot covers, stuffed them into the airlock's disposal unit, and hurried inside to find the enzymatic cleaner. She'd have to get the mud cleaned up ASAP. Bits of grass and Gaia-knew-what-else were imbedded in the prints. Armed with the enzyme jug and a sponge, she started the engines and put the vehicle back in gear. Then she turned on the vehicle's air disinfection system. The cabin would stink of ozone and chlorine, but it was better than dying.

As she set to work on the mud, she calmed down enough to wonder if anything had been stolen or tampered with. The intruder wouldn't have had much time. She scanned the cabin. The pantry cabinet was open; a half-dozen meal packets were gone, as was one of her penlights. She relaxed; it was no great loss, since she'd be getting another supply drop in just a few days.

She'd heard stories about robbers who preyed on survey vehicles near cities. More commonly, though, they intercepted supply drops instead of confronting the well-armored vehicles directly. The Sisters tagged all their equipment and supplies with tiny electronic IDs, which robbers would promptly remove once they got the chance to go over their loot. But enough slipped under the notice of thieves to allow some stolen items to be traced and their fences arrested.

Cordelia glanced at her sleeping pod. Her bear was gone.

Her heart thudded, and she felt her cheeks go hot. The bear was gone, and with it, all that was left of her husband. This was what she had *wanted*, wasn't it? To be rid of it, once and for all, so she'd stop re-living the past and get on with what life she could manage in the present?

"Yes, for the best," she muttered, even though tears were welling in her eyes. "I'll...when I get to San Francisco, I'll go out, and I'll meet someone. I'm still young enough, Sam always said I was pretty, and so I'll meet someone, somewhere, and we'll...oh *shit*."

She felt an orgasm of sorrow surging in her, and pressed hard against her eyes to stop the tears from spilling out. Who would want to be with *her*? She was pledged to serve Gaia, tied to her roving hermitage. What kind of a relationship could she have if she'd only be in town once a year? All she could expect was a night or two with a stranger.

A few teaspoons of semen, no matter how enthusiastically delivered, weren't going to fill the aching void in her soul.

No point in crying, she told herself fiercely. *It's all gone.*

Gaia's worms have Sam, a thief has the bear, and that's that. Be happy you're alive.

As the *Tortoise* lurched down the dead highway, she wondered who the robber had been. The theft tactic was unusual, and amateurish. When robbers decided to hit a survey vehicle, they'd commit themselves to the job. They'd roll a grenade under a tread, then storm the cabin, disable the emergency beacon, and take their time stripping the interior. Sometimes they left the Sister alive, sometimes not.

Well, amateurish or not, the thief had succeeded. She should've been more careful; she'd been so concerned about overt violence she'd never thought something like this would happen. It was well known that the Sisters didn't keep much in their cabins, but what they had was well-made and likely to fetch a good price on the black market.

Cold, sickening realization dawned on her. The thief, once he realized what was on the bear's VR unit, would take it to Houston and sell it to the highest bidder. And then the recording would be up for grabs across the 'Net. Her most personal and cherished memories would be laid bare to anyone with a few grubby dollars.

"Over my fucking dead body," she heard herself say.

She went to the console and re-programmed the navigation system to go back to the sabotage site.

In the few minutes it took to backtrack, she cleaned up the rest of the mud, stripped off her gloves and set up the altar again.

"Dear Mother, please forgive the trespass I am about to commit," she prayed. "It's for my own purposes that I must do this, and I mean no offense to you, but if I am to serve you I must live. And I cannot live knowing that I did nothing to keep Sam from the minds of strangers."

She snuffed the incense, put the altar away, slipped on a

new env-suit and fetched the autopistol and her emergency knapsack. The pistol was a 9 mm that held twenty rounds; she'd been given cursory instruction in its use and maintenance. In addition to the usual wilderness emergency supplies, the knapsack contained a hand-held tracking unit that detected the ID tags. Sisters were not supposed to try to retrieve minor stolen items, but the church mothers realized that sometimes a Sister would have to try to retrieve critical equipment. She hadn't tagged her bear, but the meal packs and penlight had a tag apiece.

She strapped on the gun and the knapsack, then pulled on a fresh pair of gauntlets and boot covers. She was taking an insane risk, but the thought of someone else playing the recording made her frantic with anger and embarrassment.

Cordelia found a set of footprints in the grass leading away toward the arroyo. Her hand-held scanner wasn't picking anything up yet, but it only had a range of a mile. But the thief hadn't taken much care to hide the trail. Was it carelessness? Bravado? A trap?

She swallowed down her fears and followed the prints down to the arroyo, where they skirted the high weeds at the edge of the bank. Sunning lizards fled her footsteps. The trail continued a quarter mile to a small bridge crossing the muddy remains of the creek. The bridge was primitive but sturdy, constructed from rough-trimmed mesquite branches nailed together into a walkway and railing over crude pillars of cement-mortared limestone. It looked like it had been there for many years, but it was also clear someone was maintaining it.

Cordelia was halfway over the bridge when her scanner started beeping. Not far now. She quickened her pace, and when she cleared the head-high weeds on the other side of the bank, she saw she was at the edge of a dried-up field that had probably once grown cotton or soybeans. A mile beyond sat the wreck of a barn with a collapsed roof and a sprawling limestone farm house, run-down but still intact.

She hung back. There was no way she could approach the house without being seen. The thief hadn't tried to kill her at the *Tortoise*, but now she was showing up on his doorstep. She'd be easy pickings for anyone with a scope and a high-powered rifle.

No. There was no help for it. She hadn't walked all this way just to turn back now.

She began to plod across the field, startling a jackrabbit taking a siesta beneath a tumbleweed. The sun was rising high in the sky, and the morning cool was giving way to oppressive heat. It was becoming hard to breathe inside the muggy suit, hard to see past the perspiration running into her eyes. Sweat ran in an itchy, incessant drip down the groove of her back. The damned env-suit must have been designed by the same people who made the little microwave stew bags in her ration packs.

Cordelia marched on, keeping her eyes fixed on the farmhouse. She more than half expected to see a muzzle flash from one of the dark windows and feel the wet, hot pain of a bullet punching into her chest, her stomach, her forehead.

But the flash never came. Soon, she was standing under a broad oak tree in the front yard, gasping for breath and trying fruitlessly to wipe her eyes through her headgear.

The scanner was beeping frantically now, registering three distinct signals. Her supplies were here, all right. No one had come out to accost her yet; could it be that the thief had simply deposited the loot here and left? Not likely; as far as Cordelia could tell, there wasn't anywhere else to go.

With shaking hands, Cordelia unsnapped her holster and

drew the pistol. The single-story limestone house looked to be about a hundred years old; the rock walls still looked solid. Most of the windows were broken and were either boarded up or curtained in rags. The front door hung loosely on green-rusted brass hinges. The roof was shingled with a patchwork of tarred plywood boards, homemade mesquite shingles, and thatches of tarred straw.

Was the thief a squatter? Or a descendant of the original household? A very, very few people had an inheritable immunity to the panvirus, but the genetics behind that immunity had proved too complex to create a genetic therapy.

Cordelia crept up the limestone steps and pushed open the creaky front door. As her eyes adjusted to the dimness, she thumbed up the threshold on her scanner. Finally her vision cleared, revealing the tattered remains of carpet and worn wooden furniture. Holding the scanner in front of her with her left hand, she stepped inside, keeping her pistol tucked ready against her side with her right. She swept the scanner from side to side.

Beep beep beep beep beep.

To the right. Hugging the wall, she followed the scanner through a debris-strewn kitchen and down a hallway to a small, tidy, sunlit bedroom. The room was furnished with a small antique vanity and a single bed with a faded floral bedspread; the empty wrappers of two meal packs lay beside a burlap sack in the middle of the bed. A low, wide table beside the bed was crowded with a dozen dolls and stuffed animals, all surprisingly clean. Her teddy bear sat at the front of the pack, black eyes glittering expectantly.

Cordelia put her pistol away and stepped forward to retrieve her bear.

"Quien eres?"

Cordelia spun around, clumsily drawing her pistol. A red-haired, freckled girl of about eighteen or nineteen stood in the doorway, a butcher knife clenched in her left hand. Her ragged, muddy jeans and tee shirt hung loose on a lean body toughened by work and sun. The girl flinched when she saw Cordelia's gun, but she did not flee.

"Quien eres?" the girl repeated, voice shaky.

"Soy Cordelia," she replied. It had been a long time since she'd spoken the language. She used to chat with the old Cuban women at the corner grocery store in Philadelphia, but since she'd been with the Sisters, her tongue had curled around nothing but English.

"This is mine." Cordelia continued in Spanish, pointing at the bear. "I have come to take it back. Why did you steal it from me?"

"I only wanted food," the girl stammered hoarsely, letting the knife drop. She seemed to be searching for words as much as Cordelia was. "It has not rained for months. Nothing grows but cactus. I was digging for toads in the arroyo when I heard your machine. I meant only to take the food, but when I saw the toy...it is so much nicer than anything I have. I meant no harm."

The pleading, anxious look in the girl's hazel eyes spoke volumes. *I have been alone so terribly long.*

"What's your name?" Cordelia asked gently, lowering the pistol. "Where are your people?"

"My name's Sonja. I haven't got any people, not any more. Papa died from the sickness before I was born. Mama raised me. A snake bit her in the leg when we were hunting deer when I was seven. I couldn't suck the poison out in time."

"I'm sorry."

"Mama...mama said everyone else in the camp where she met Papa died from the sickness. Is that why you're wearing... that white thing? Are you sick?"

"No. I'm fine. But the sickness is everywhere. I was afraid you'd be infected."

"The sickness never took hold here; that's why Mama brought me here." The girl paused. "Are there many people left?"

"Not as many as before. A few million, I think. Enough to re-build the cities."

The girl took a shuddering breath. Cordelia realized Sonja was crying.

"I dream of cities," Sonja said, tears running down her face. "I dream of people who smile and talk to me and touch me, but when I wake there's nothing but the sun and the sound of the wind in the grass. I don't want to be alone. Please, take me with you."

Cordelia was silent for a moment. She couldn't very well leave the girl here, but could she really take her along? It could be that the area wasn't infected...but it could also be that the girl was naturally immune. And therefore a host.

Cordelia looked into the girl's pleading eyes. No. She couldn't abandon her. With all the technology aboard the *Tortoise*, there *had* to be a way to get the girl to civilization safely.

"All right. Get your things," Cordelia said.

Cordelia had to severely limit what Sonja wanted to take. In the end, the girl toted two big burlap sacks; the first contained the bear and the meals she'd stolen, the second contained the girl's toy collection, a few photos, and some clean garments. None of it was likely to carry infection.

Sonja's muddy clothing, however, presented a problem.

"You have to take off your clothes and leave them out here," Cordelia said as they got to the airlock.

"I'm sorry," she added when she saw Sonja's look of dismay.

"They're too dirty. I haven't got enough disinfectant to clean them."

Sonja silently took off her sneakers, slipped off her tee shirt and shimmied out of her jeans. Cordelia tried not to look at the girl's naked body, but she couldn't help it. Sonja was beautiful, her legs long and lean, the skin of her unsunned torso a smooth, creamy pink...Cordelia made herself look away.

As they both got in the cramped airlock, Cordelia tried desperately to ignore the way the girl's body felt pressed against hers. She gave a silent prayer of thanks when the lock cycled open.

How can I think of this poor girl this way? she wondered miserably as Sonja dropped her sacks by the door.

Cordelia went to the console and put the *Tortoise* back in motion. *She probably sees an old woman when she looks at me. A dirty old woman.*

"We need to get you cleaned up," Cordelia said, realizing that wouldn't be enough to let her take her env-suit off. But the less dirt in the cabin, the better. "The bathroom is over there in the corner."

The bathroom was one of the Tortoise's most ingenious space-saving designs. The whole thing was a shower stall, the walls molded from seamless white antimicrobial plastic. On one wall was a chest-high basin for brushing teeth or washing hair. The other wall had a toilet that, when the watertight cover was in place, served nicely as a bathing stool. The third wall facing the door held soap dispensers, and the ceiling held the low-flow shower head, overhead light, and several dryer vents. The *Tortoise* had enough recyclable water for her to take twenty minutes of showers each week.

Cordelia hadn't showered in a few days; she liked to save up so she could have a really satisfying, hot shower instead of a two-minute rinse-off. The tank should be full enough to get Sonja thoroughly scrubbed off.

"What is all this?" Sonja asked wonderingly, peering into the bathroom at the strange fixtures. "How do I work this?"

"You, well..." Cordelia trailed off. She'd had to read a five-page manual before she got the hang of the bathroom system. If she tried to talk the girl through it, she'd run out of water before she was halfway done. And the bathroom *was* big enough for two people. "Oh, hell, I should just show you."

Cordelia shooed Sonja inside and shut the door behind them. "Okay, first the water..." she waved her hand in front of the shower head to turn it on. "...a little cold, it'll get warm fast. Solar heat's a beautiful thing. Now we get some soap by pressing this button here...yeah, now soap yourself good, all over. Get your neck, you've got some mud behind your ear."

She could barely feel the wonderful hot water through her env-suit, and her faceplate was fogging up again. The situation was just so many shades of wrong that Cordelia wanted to cry. Would she really have to stay in this damned suit forever?

Then she realized the girl was staring at her. Sonja's nipples had gone hard in the spray.

"Are you sure I'll make you sick?" the girl asked. She gently touched Cordelia's faceplate. "Can't you take this off? Don't you want a shower, too?" She paused, blushing. "I—I want to see what you look like."

Cordelia's heart was pounding, and she felt as dizzy as if she'd been breathing ether.

If I can't smell the flowers or feel the sun, then what's the point?

Before she'd fully realized what she was doing, she'd broken the seal on her env-suit and was pulling off her headgear. As she took her first breath of steamy, soap-and-Sonja-scented air, she briefly thought she'd fall dead on the spot.

Not dead yet, she thought. *May as well do this right and die clean.*

Cordelia pulled off the rest of her suit, then unzipped her jumper and boots and slipped out of them and her underwear. She opened the door enough to kick the sodden wad of clothing out into the cabin, then turned back to face Sonja.

Seeing the girl like this for the first time with naked eyes and body made Cordelia unspeakably aroused. The itchy fire in her vagina was almost unbearable. She swallowed nervously and tried to keep her face impassive.

"Well, this is me."

Cordelia reached past Sonja for the soap, and the girl caught Cordelia's hand. To her amazement, Cordelia realized that the girl's eyes shone with lust.

"Touch me," the girl whispered.

Cordelia was rooted to the spot, terrified at the thought of actually touching a real live horny human being. A virgin, no less, not even raised by wolves. This girl hadn't had any human contact for most of her life, hadn't ever been on a date or been hugged or kissed by a lover. And Cordelia hadn't even *done* this before, not with another woman—what if she screwed up?

Sonja put Cordelia's hand against her breast and held it there. The touch of the girl's firm flesh under her palm was an electric shock that drove away her fears. The girl's heart was beating fast as a bird's. Cordelia pulled Sonja to her and kissed her fiercely, ran her fingers over the girl's wet auburn tangles with her free hand.

As they explored each other's mouths with lips and tongues, Cordelia ran her hands over the girl's smooth curves. She ran her free hand down the girl's belly to her curling dark pubic hair. Sonja kissed her harder, squeezing her hand, moaning into her mouth. Cordelia cupped her vulva with her hand, then ran the tip of her finger up the girl's wet groove to her clit.

The girl broke off the kiss with a cry.

"Oh God, it *burns!*" Sonja gasped.

Cordelia slowly circled the clit with her fingers. "Do you want me to kiss you down here?"

The girl nodded, speechless, and released Cordelia's hand.

Cordelia sat down on the toilet lid and drew Sonja closer 'til the girl's vulva was inches from her face. She gently spread the girl's quivering thighs and breathed on the swollen pink flesh.

"Oh God." Sonja's voice was barely a squeak.

Cordelia parted her labia with her left thumb. The girl's clit was fully engorged, the little acorn of flesh nearly purple. She found the girl's vagina with her other hand. Her hymen was tight, but there was just enough room for a finger. Sonja's body was rigid and shivering. Very slowly, she slid her index finger into her and licked her clit.

The young woman cried out, and Cordelia felt her muscles shudder around her finger. She pressed her tongue against the girl's flesh to sustain the orgasm, as Sam had often done for her when she'd come before he could enter her.

Finally, Cordelia released Sonja, and she slid down the wet plastic wall to sit dazed by the drain. They'd run out of water, and the dryers had come on.

"Are...are you a man?" the girl asked uncertainly.

"No. I'm not a man," Cordelia replied gently. "I'm a woman. Like you."

Cordelia paused. "Did you like what I did to you?"

The girl nodded.

"Do you think you could do it to me?"

Another nod.

Several hours later, Sonja lay asleep in Cordelia's arms on

the bunk. The low vibrations from the Tortoise's engines rocked them gently. Cordelia was deliciously exhausted, but didn't want to sleep, not yet. She wanted to savor the moment before it was gone.

She stroked Sonja's still-wet hair. San Francisco. Would she make it? For all she knew, she was infected now, and likely to die in a few weeks, maybe even a few days. She'd have to prepare Sonja for the worst, show her how to work the control console and the communications equipment. The girl probably didn't know how to read, and obviously didn't know English. Cordelia could teach her, before they got to San Francisco, if she had time...

No. It wasn't possible. They couldn't go to San Francisco and risk infecting everyone in the city. They'd have to go back to Sonja's farmhouse. She could keep the supplies and radio and put the *Tortoise* on autopilot to send it back to home base. If Cordelia died, Sonja would still have her toys and her home. And if Cordelia lived...maybe they could build a good life together out here in the wilderness. And if the area proved to be virus-free, others could join them. Cordelia knew the road ahead would be hard, but it would be worth it.

She kissed Sonja's forehead and slipped out of bed without waking the girl. Cordelia pulled on her boots, and opened up the airlock.

She stepped naked into the light from the setting sun. She could feel the cool evening breeze on her bare skin, smell the flowers and earth that had been denied her for so long. She fell to her knees on the dew-damp grass and breathed in the world. Yes. The smell of a flower, the feel of mud beneath her hands, the touch of a beautiful girl...it was all worth dying for.

Finally, after she'd watched the sun set below the horizon, she got up and headed back into the *Tortoise*. Sonja still lay sleeping, hugging Cordelia's pillow to her chest. Cordelia got out Gaia's altar and began to pray for life.

Part Three:
Random Play

Stripping in the Midwest

THERE'S SOMETHING SURREAL about sitting on a couch watching a professional porn video with the person *in* that video sitting right beside you.

I've known since I met her (and her husband) that "Satine" works as a stripper and wants to do girl-girl video work. But until I was invited to watch her first video appearance, I'd only seen stray topless photos.

Imagine a svelte woman with short auburn hair and pert, pink breasts. She's strapped naked to benches and chained in wooden cages, gazing sultry at the camera. Her pussy is shaved, her legs long and smooth as ivory. She's a little bit goth, a little bit cabaret. Now imagine her dressed in nothing but stiletto heels and long vinyl gloves, dominating a busty LA blonde with a cat-o-nine-tails.

"One of the great things about my job is all the female performers I get to meet," she says. "Ladies like Nina Hartley and Jenna Jameson. I recently got to know Kobe Tai, who is incredibly sweet and puts on a hell of a feature show."

For Satine, stripping and erotic modeling are a simple economic decision. She's intelligent, but she hasn't got a college degree. And she has the looks and body and utter lack of self-consciousness required to dance naked for an audience.

Before she did stripping full-time, she worked as a tech

support rep for a local telecom company. After she quit that job, she told me, "Tech support made me feel *far* more degraded than taking off my clothes in front of strangers does. I got yelled at and cursed by customers all the time. I absolutely hated humanity when I left that job at the end of the day...and I didn't make that much money. After I started stripping, it was no contest which one I'd rather do."

On a *bad* night of stripping, she tells me, she makes around $300. Good nights have netted her over $1000, generally when a guy with a lot of money to burn rounds up two or three dancers for long private dancing sessions in the Champagne Room. On her best night, she came home with $1500 in fat, sweaty rolls of ones and fives and tens stuffed in her denim overalls. Not bad for a woman with a high school diploma.

But all that was totally peripheral as I got to know her. I'd met her husband first through an online horror writers' board—and ironically he and Satine turned out to live in my apartment complex, less than fifty yards from my own door. So I'd go over to their apartment or vice versa and we'd talk about writing and comics. We'd all watch science fiction movies and *Farscape* and old *Twilight Zone* episodes. Satine would putter around the house in jeans or sweats, herding cats or baking chocolate chip cookies.

So I never really saw her as anything but a fellow geek. She doesn't adhere to any of the negative stereotypes about strippers: she doesn't have breast implants, doesn't tan, doesn't bleach her hair, and isn't an alcoholic or a drug abuser. She isn't a flirt, and she doesn't wear especially revealing clothes when she's not onstage.

She doesn't like to take unnecessary risks. She always has her imposingly-built husband pick her up and drop her off, and he carries a stun gun (which unfortunately he's had to use). He chaperones her at any private dances or photo shoots.

Stripping isn't an easy job. The dancing is physically demanding, and too often the patrons are on their absolute worst behavior. Curses, derogatory comments, and having to endure overwhelmingly foul body odor are not uncommon. She's also been licked, slapped and bitten (all of which, she says, is still better than tech support).

Satine once told me, "If engaged women could see how their husbands-to-be act in here toward women during bachelor parties, a lot of future divorces could be avoided, because those marriages just wouldn't happen."

However, she notes that bisexual women are often grabbier than men during a lapdance. "Bi girls who come in with their boyfriends seem to think that, because they're female, it's okay to touch us. And it isn't."

She pauses, then smiles slyly. "Not that I'd really *mind* some of these girls touching me. To see some hot young thing wanting so *bad* to touch me, wanting to put her hands on my tits, to slip her fingers under my g-string and feel my pussy... yeah. It's fun to watch their faces, to imagine what they'd like to do to me. I like seeing people sweat when I'm dancing between their knees. But you have to follow the rules, and touching the dancers is a no-no."

By contrast, she says that butch-seeming lesbian customers are typically the best-behaved and most likely to keep their hands to themselves.

Satine says she has a few regulars who are her favorite customers. "These guys just want someone to keep them company while they drink. One of my regulars might give me $50-$100 in tips to sit and talk to him for a while; he never asks for lapdances, and he never tries to get me to drink alcohol."

The club has a complex payment system, and in order to avoid getting cheated by the house, a dancer has to pay attention and have a reasonably good business sense. Strippers are not employees of the club per se—they are all treated as independent contractors. That means they have to take care of their own health insurance and federal deductions for income tax and social security (of course, this leaves them a lot of leeway on what they decide to declare as income).

At the end of each night, the dancer owes a certain percentage of her money (based on the number of dances she's logged) as tips to the bouncers, DJs, and to the "house mom". A dancer may also owe fines for breaking certain house rules. For instance, at Satine's club, if a dancer chooses not to go out and work the floor during "up time" (a sort of "happy hour" for lapdances in the club's main room) she gets fined $10, which goes partly to the DJ and partly to the house.

There are also lots of pitfalls to avoid. Club managers will often encourage young dancers to participate in "after hours" private parties, where drugs and alcohol will flow freely and the dancers will be pressured to have sex, whether onstage or with patrons, for money.

She fully agrees that there's a lot of truth to the widely-accepted stereotypes about strippers. She's told me that a lot of the girls who've worked at the clubs she's worked are stripping because they lack the intelligence or discipline to get into or stay in college. Many strippers start out as alcoholics or end up that way. And so many of the other girls have children out of wedlock that she says her customers often don't believe her when she tells them she doesn't have kids.

But on the other hand, she's known dancers who are extremely together. "There's one girl at my club who's 20, owns her own house, holds down a regular day job in addition to stripping, and has guardianship over her niece and nephew. I know people twice her age who couldn't handle that kind of responsibility."

The club where Satine works is widely agreed to be the classiest strip joint in town and is the one most often visted by celebrities. Satine met Keanu Reeves there and got to do dances for Harrison Ford (she got his signature on a Champagne Room cocktail napkin, which she promptly framed).

Her working at the club also got her involved with Playboy Video's "Strip Search" series. Talent scouts for Playboy came to the club last year and recruited Satine and several other girls to do a video shoot in a full-nude club in Dayton, OH.

As a result of the Playboy videos, I finally saw Satine do her thing. Her husband cued up the first tape, and several mutual friends and I watched in rapt embarrassment as Satine was interviewed with another girl. Satine seemed to have lost about 40 IQ points. The vacuous, vampy, vinyl-clad vixen on the screen surely wasn't the same girl sitting beside me, was she? Then video-Satine and the other girl were on a bed, kissing, spanking, biting.

"She hit me really hard, there," Satine noted as the other girl whaled on her bare derriere with a leather paddle. "I had a bruise for a week."

Her husband put in the second tape. Video-Satine strutted down the catwalk in a slinky black vinyl dress and a pair of nasty boots, then proceeded to divest herself of said accoutrements. I wondered, as she writhed naked on the stage floor, if she ever had the urge to rub her entire body down in hand sanitizer after she got off work (I later learned that she keeps a big pump bottle of the stuff in her locker).

Video-Satine continued to writhe and grind for the hooting frat boy types seated near her. The cameraman went in for the close-up of her pink bits.

Satine sat up, leaning toward the screen at her vulva.

"Huh," she said. "I never knew I had a mole there."

Indeed, stripping has been a true journey of self-discovery.

How Linux Boy Met the Mistress of the Beast with Two Backs

HOW MUCH GUS could a succubus buss if a succubus could buss Gus?

Every last bit of him.

Gus Wiebel was my housemate/landlord back at MIT. Gus was an übergeek among geeks; he'd made a tidy wad of cash off a first-person shooter he coded for a local software firm in the late 90s. So, he bought a huge double in Somerville, MA, knocked out the walls between the units and turned it into a big rooming house for his friends.

Gus liked having people around, but he was really shy and introverted. He would sit up in his room at his triple-monitor computer working on code or playing games and munching on Captain Crunch and getting very round. People started calling him Resident Weevil.

It was about evenly split between guys and girls in the house, and the number of resident geeks ranged from 10 to 15 depending on who was broke and needed a cheap place for the semester and who finally got sick of the mess and moved out. Most of the people in the house had the social skills of spastic groundhogs. As a result, hardly anyone ever got laid.

All that changed the night of Gus' 21st birthday. Rajiv, a grad student who was the most outgoing person in the house, dragged Gus to Manray to ogle the goth chicks in their corsets and fishnets. I still have no idea how Raj convinced Gus to go out; he must've offered to buy him single malt scotches 'til he was swimming.

While they went to the club, a bunch of us were downstairs watching anime. My housemate Betty had brought her friend Susan by. I'd always liked Betty, but the housemate thing made us getting into anything more than friendship kind of awkward. Susan was this tall, auburn-haired music major at U. Mass. She was screamingly babalicious, but she had no idea of her own beauty. We'd talked before, but the sight of her made my tongue knot in my mouth. I'm sure I sounded like a grade-A doofus. I had no clue how to ask her out; I'd probably get shot down like a hang glider going up against an F-22.

So I sat there in the dark, not two feet from this beautiful girl, pretending to watch Evangelion while all I wanted to do was to lose myself in the green sea of her eyes.

Around 3 a.m. the front door opened. In walked this stunning woman leading Rajiv and our Resident Weevil by their hands. Raj and Gus had that stupid happy dazed look that young guys get when they're a bit drunk and have just gotten lucky chickwise beyond their wildest expectations.

And this woman...man, Raj and Gus could've never expected to land a lady like her. She was so hot, I expected the carpet to start smoking under her feet. I wondered for a split-second if Gus had bought an escort, but as I watched the lady lead them around like a couple of stoned puppies, I knew that cash was too simple a thing for her to be interested in. The way she carried herself and seemed to look right through you—this woman was in control.

I couldn't help but stare at her—and neither could anyone else in the room, I soon realized. Every eye was on her. And she knew it. She gave us all this knowing Mona Lisa smile as she led Raj and Gus to the staircase. I felt myself getting hard; she was absolutely radiating sex.

She was halfway up the stairs, almost out of sight of the living room, when she reached into her handbag and pulled out a handful of small objects in brightly colored plastic wrappers.

At first I thought she had Halloween candy. Then she tossed the handful down to us, calling, "Have fun, kids!" as she disappeared upstairs with Raj and Gus.

One piece of "candy" landed on my head, and I realized she'd thrown us all a handful of condoms. There was a scent coming off the wrapper, the scent of roses, and it made me so hard I could hardly stand it.

And then Susan practically tackled me. She grabbed me by the back of my shirt and spun me around so she could plant this amazing kiss on me. I could feel her nipples had gone rock-hard under her blouse. She was tugging at my tee shirt, trying to pull it off over my head. I helped her, and then she pushed me back onto the carpet, straddled me, and started to work at my fly.

"S-susan," I began.

"Don't talk," she whispered hoarsely. "Just fuck me, Linux boy."

Who was I to argue? I relaxed and let her undress me, and in that moment I realized everyone in the room was getting their freak on. Little mousy Wai-Chen was giving big shaggy Bart a blow job. Paul had got Amanda up on top of the television set and was giving her a tongue lashing she'd probably never forget.

And then my housemate Betty came over; she'd stripped completely naked, and had a slightly mad gleam in her eye.

"If someone doesn't get me off soon, I'm going to explode all over this entire room," she said.

"Well, my tongue's not busy," I found myself saying. "Want

a ride?"

Indeed she did.

If this was heaven, I'd be glad to die.

The three of us had mad, glorious sex in the living room all night long. When morning came, we were sticky and rug-burned and sore and very, very happy. I think we'd all fallen in love with each other.

The bunch of us decided to go out for breakfast, so I went upstairs to find out if Raj and Gus wanted to go, too. I found them in Raj's room; Raj was sprawled on the bed, and Gus was wrapped in a sheet on the floor. The window was open, and the woman was gone.

They were sleeping so hard that at first I thought they were in a coma. I was worried they'd OD'ed on something, so I called Betty and Susan. We got them awake, but they were groggy and weak. But *happy*. Whatever the woman—they said her name was Lilith—had done to them, she'd blown cocks and minds alike.

They told us some of it at breakfast. As they tossed back coffee and plowed through plates of eggs and waffles, they told us how she'd gotten them doing stuff to her and each other they hadn't thought possible. She'd shown them positions and nerve points they'd never read about in any book or seen in any porno movie. She opened the doors to sexual secrets mortals were not meant to know.

As mind-blowing as my night with Betty and Susan had been, I have to say I was still envious. Even though I could see she'd taken something from them—their hair started coming in gray after that—I still wished I'd been the one she'd found and chosen.

That night changed Raj and Gus forever. Their weakness passed after a few days, and after that they started fixing up the house. Out went the junk and trashed furniture; in came drapes and cool rugs and soft furniture and a wet bar. They got decent haircuts and new clothes and hired a maid.

We didn't play World of Warcraft anymore; everyone was too busy gettin' busy. Gus and Raj started working on virtual reality sex programs for a different local firm and started making even more mad cash than before.

And me? Well, that night changed me, too. I went from being a loveless tongue-tied loser to a man who gets to keep company with two of the finest women in Boston.

If you see Lilith, be sure to thank her for me.

How To Get A Goth Out of a Tree (An alternative to cutting the rope)

TEDDY WAS UP on a low limb of the oak, clinging to the trunk and sobbing in terror. His thin body trembled in the cold moonlight. He'd broken two of his carefully manicured, black-lacquered fingernails. His mascara was running down his cheeks in sticky black rivulets, and his lipstick was a dark smear across his lips.

A half-dozen clubgoers were gathered nearby, staring up at him curiously, helplessly. A couple seemed irritated. None were doing anything to get him out of the damn tree.

"Teddy?" I called, stepping toward him through the crusty snow. "What's the matter?"

"Stop it!" he shrieked. His pupils were hugely dilated. "Bunnies! You're h-h-hurting the bunnies!"

He began to wail loudly, so loudly that anyone within a five-block radius was bound to hear. The cops would surely come if we didn't get him down and get him quiet. His sister would never forgive us if he wound up in jail.

I turned to Rose, who was puffing on a clove cigarette.

"What the hell is he on?" I asked her. "Acid?"

She blinked at me behind her silver granny glasses. "Uh uh. I think he took a bunch of motion sickness pills."

"Scopolamine?" I asked.

"I guess. He's tripping balls," she added helpfully.

Sigh.

I began to walk toward Teddy more slowly, picking up my skirts and stepping carefully around imaginary rabbits.

"What do you see, Teddy?"

"B-bunnies. Pink bunnies. All over the ground. They bust when you step on them. Got b-bunny guts a-all over me," he hiccupped.

"There's no bunnies," I said gently. "Come down from there. You're going to catch your death up there. You're ruining your fishnets on the bark."

He shook his head, his eyes wide. "Don' wanna hurt the bunnies."

Shit.

I walked back through the parking lot to the club. The Project Pitchfork song thudding within made the pebbles near the door jump with every bass beat.

"Sorry, can't let you back in," the bouncer said.

"I don't want back in," I replied. "I just want to borrow Osiris for a couple of minutes." I pulled ten dollars out of my pocket. "Do you think you could find him for me? It's kind of an emergency."

Osiris' real name was Shaquim Johnson. His father had briefly played as a middle linebacker for the Chicago Bears, and was deeply disappointed that his only son had no interest in sports aside from some casual weightlifting.

The bouncer took my money and disappeared into the club. A few minutes later, Osiris emerged, stooping low to get through the door. When he straightened up, I was staring at him in his leather-clad solar plexus.

"What's up?" he asked. He had the kind of deep voice you imagine gods having.

"Teddy's freaked out and climbed a tree. He's yelling so

much, I'm scared he'll bring the cops. Can you get him down and get him to our van? Please?"

"No problem." He flashed me a dazzling white smile, and strode across the snow to the gaggle of goths around the tree. His hobnail boots left prints bigger than my head.

Teddy shrieked when he saw Osiris approaching. "No, not the Candyman! I didn't eat that fish!"

Unperturbed, Osiris lifted Teddy out of the tree, slung him over his shoulder, and carried him to Rose's minivan.

We bundled Teddy under a blanket, gave him a piece of bubble wrap to play with, then piled in around him to take him back to his sister's house in Urbana.

"Bunnies," he whispered. "Poor little bunnies."

It was going to be a long drive home.

True Romance

The fancy Valentine's dinner
of chard and broccoli amandine
hits your innards at bedtime and
urgently you are the expanding
woman, Frau Hindenburg,
tethered under silken sheets.

You try a little release, a teeny
mouse's squeak, nothing more
but it's a noxious foghorn
that makes the dog sneeze,
doves are dying in the trees and
in high heaven, Baby Jesus weeps.

Then Husband comes in, his passion
withering in the lingering pong,
and he gasps, "What is *that*?"
Eyes watery, you look down demurely
at the dog and say, "I think Scout
ate that bacon we tossed out."

Hearing his name, the scraphound
wags at you, his Judas mistress,
and stirs the stench a little more.
Your husband nods gravely, wobbly,
and shoos the beast from the bedroom
while you wedge open the window.

It's not a trip down denial
that he managed to marry
a gassy finger-crossing minx;
it's that the air will clear itself
more easily than clouded dignity
and he loves you, farts and all.

<u>Fragment</u>

WE NEED TO GET you a girlfriend." Rita kissed me on the tip of my nose and rolled off the bed.

I watched her Valentine heart-shaped derriere as she knelt to gather our discarded toys and then padded into the bathroom.

"But you're my girlfriend. Right?" I replied.

"Of course I am." Her tone was light, but there was a tension in her voice that made my heart sink.

"Then why do I need another one?" I managed to keep my voice steady.

"I think it would be better if you found someone in your own city," she said. "Someone who would be closer to you. Someone more available than me."

I stretched my arm across the still-warm space on the bed where she'd been. The black cotton was smooth and comforting under my fingertips. Black was a good color for cocktail dresses and leather jackets; it wasn't a practical color for bedclothes. Rita's husband Lenny did their laundry, and I knew he would come back from his date with Mark, drop his jaw comically and exclaim, "Great Scott, what have you ladies done to my sheets?"

I climbed off the bed and went into the bathroom. Rita was washing off our toys, neatly lining the silicone cocks up in a row on a hand towel to dry: red, purple, blue. I slipped my arms around her waist and kissed the nape of her neck. The smell of her set my heart racing again; touching her naked skin was like plugging myself into a gentle electric current.

We'd known each other for years; we both went to the same summer writing workshop, and then kept running into each other at conferences. I knew from the first moment I saw her that there was something I really liked about her. But I'd never been with a woman; despite being polyamorous, she hadn't, either. At one conference we'd both had a bit to drink and were both riding the high of having made some excellent story sales and before I knew it we were kissing in the elevator at 2am. And then we went back to her room.

It's a cliché to say that I felt like a virgin all over again, but I did. And it was like a new door in my soul had been opened, a room where I was the best, happiest person I could hope to be, and only Rita held the key to it. I'd fallen in love before, but never like this; it was as if every molecule in every cell of my body became tuned to the sound of her heartbeat, her breathing. I didn't feel truly alive except when I was in her arms. I didn't care that she was married; I didn't care that she had other partners. All I wanted was the chance to be with her, to have my moments of pure joy, to have the chance to love her.

"Why would it be better?" I could feel that perfect jewel of happiness inside me start to fragment. "Things have been fine, haven't they?"

She smiled at me in the mirror, but quickly looked away. "I'm not making as many sales as I was, and Lenny and I need to cut back on our travel expenses. I don't know when I can get out to see you again."

"I can keep coming here—"

"It's not fair to you to have to do that."

"I don't mind. I love you," I said.

"I know you do." She bit her lip, not meeting my gaze in our reflection. "But...I can't be your only lover. It's too much pressure."

She paused for an agonizingly long beat before she spoke again: "You were my first. You'll always be special to me..."

I let my arms fall from her waist, "...just not that special?"

In the hanging silence, all I could hear was my own heart pounding. How could something so completely shattered continue to beat so smoothly? I wondered if I might drop dead right there on her tile floor. I held my breath, hoping for oblivion, but it never came to rescue me. In some alternate universe, I had fallen to my knees, sobbing inconsolably, clinging to her legs, begging her *Please please tell me what I did wrong I'll do anything to make things better I just want to be with you please*, but in this universe I had gone completely numb and was still as a corpse.

The silver lining to abject shock is you get to keep some of your dignity.

"I'm sorry," she finally said.

"Me, too."

The Dominatrix Confesses

MY FATHER WAS a mean drunk. He didn't indulge often, but when he did, evil came out. *Way* out. Once the tears had dried and the doors and chairs were repaired, my mother would tell me stories of relatives who died well before I was born—the smart, charming ones on her side of the family drank themselves to death before they turned 40.

I worried that I might have inherited the family genes for alcoholism. I barely drank at all before I was 25 or so, wondering if I'd have that second sip and suddenly find myself unable to stop until the bottle was empty. I was scared that I would drink and get drunk and totally lose control. Violence can be hot, yeah...but not like that. Never like that. Sloppy mean isn't sexy. And the mean drunks I've known are *always* mean—they just hide it when they're sober, because they have to.

I have learned, since then, that I have nothing to fear from alcohol. One and I'm done. I don't crave more. There's no liquor-fiending beast inside me.

Love, on the other hand...a little is never enough for me.

One kiss and I want more and more and more. I want to be closer. I wish I didn't have to use those gloves and condoms. I wish I could taste my lovers in every way possible.

Three days with someone I love, breathing them, drinking them, and my body is addicted. And they leave to return home, and my hormones are crashing hard. It's an emotional hangover. Love can be intellectual, it can be sexual, but for me it is also chemical. Chemical and primal and while I am in its grip I am bound.

That knowledge doesn't make the crash any easier, but at least I can manage it a bit better. And I have people in my life who are perfectly willing to provide emotional aftercare as long as I mostly behave myself. Just because I'm on fire doesn't mean I shouldn't keep the whole house from burning down.

I can show you whips, chains, nipple clamps, all that and a side of lube. Those things are just thrills. They don't really scare anyone, not when I'm holding them. But love? My kind of love? That's a different story.

I learned the hard way that I shouldn't talk about my feelings when I am in love. They are too scary for most people who don't feel the things I do, or at least don't feel them with the same intensity. So even when I'm naked, I keep my heart behind black glass.

I don't care so much if my lovers can't reflect back the same feelings I have; surely that is a sign of the addiction for me. If I were truly a proud domme I would hold out until I found someone who burned as I burn. I would wait for those who love as hard as they can.

I would wait for a banquet in heaven instead of eating my own ashes in hell.

But I would be waiting a long damn time, wouldn't I?

And I would be dying of hunger.

I am hungry.

I want more.

I don't want to stop.

Don't be afraid, little girl. Don't be afraid, little boy. I will keep my fire to myself and I promise I won't burn you.

<u>Cougar</u>

Respect. I got boots older than you, boy,

so don't say the c-word like it's bad.
I know what I'm doing. Do you?
You say you want some sweet young
thing, her head full of fluffy-dovey love,
soft and forgiving, naive. No rough life
led, no diamond-hard eyes watching
you work. Rosebud beauty just lies
there and sweats while you wish
for a lover who'll bend your pride
to her knee, thrill you and show
you everything they can't capture
on glossy paper or film or magnetic
tape. You can't do better than your own
imagination if your friends all have staples.
My flesh is real, but it's my mind
you want, even if you don't know it yet.

Respect. I got scars older than you, boy.

Wanna see?

The Lonely Ones Will Find Each Other by the Heat of Their Bodies

YOU'RE IN A STRANGE CITY. It's dark and cold, and you're so ravenously hungry that you think you're going to faint at any moment. Your pockets are stuffed full of money, but you can't find a restaurant or market. Everything in this city seems to have closed for the night.

You walk and you walk, feet aching, head swimming with hunger, when finally you spot a soft neon glow in the distance. A restaurant! Salvation!

You reach the front door and try to go inside...but the maitre 'd blocks your way and pushes you back onto the steps. Is there a dress code? Is your face dirty? He won't tell you anything other than that you aren't allowed inside. He's indifferent to the cash you show him, indifferent to your pleading.

So you sit by the door outside, getting hungrier and hungrier and colder and colder, smelling all the wonderful food, hearing the warm laughter and clink of silverware on plates.

And then your friends come waddling out, stuffed to the gills, and when they see you they say, "Oh, you don't want to come in *here*, the food is just awful!"

All your life, you've yearned for a best friend, a lover, a life companion. You know it's a tall order. But it's what you need.

You need it like you need air and water...and try as you might, you just can't seem to find your love.

You were an only child, or maybe you were lost in a sea of brothers and sisters. Growing up, you were too shy and weird to make friends easily. If the other kids noticed you, it was to make fun of you. So at school, you always sat at the back of the room. Once you got big enough, your parents would just leave you at home when they went to the theater or to the dance club or to whatever Adult Stuff they did that they didn't want to drag a kid along to. And you remember sitting in your room screaming at the walls because you were so fucking lonely.

Now you're an adult, and you're still sitting in your room screaming at the walls. And, as always, nothing answers but silence.

Maybe your relationships have been brief and far between, one night stands scattered across a frigid, barren landscape.

But maybe you've been in long-term relationships. You've been in love, your heart broken so many times you're surprised it still works. And one day you wake up to realize that all the people you've ever loved are now married. After all your sweat and tears trying to get them to love you, too, after all their claims of not wanting commitment...they're committed. To someone else.

And no one can say why you lacked that certain *je ne sais quoi d'amour*, not even them.

You're a good person, and you have a lot to offer a lover. You're considerate, generous, and you have the Kama Sutra practically memorized. But you see the men going out with vacuous, whining bimbos and the women going out with jerks and slimeballs...and no one's giving you the time of day.

It's gotten so the moment you see someone you're attracted to, desire is immediately crushed by an overwhelming sense of despair from the weight of all your past rejections. And sometimes, all you feel is rage at the sight of couples holding hands, kissing, smiling at each other. "Paint it Black" becomes the soundtrack playing on an endless loop inside your mind.

Your friends—who at this point are mostly all in committed relationships—are full of helpful advice.

You particularly like the Ann Landers Special, which is: "Feeling Lonely? Get a dog!" Wow, great idea. You need someone you can have meaningful conversations with and make love with and go to the movies with and buy a house with and have kids with...yeah, a dog is the *perfect* replacement for a human being!

You also love the advice you get from older friends who are going through divorce or who are about to get a divorce. These are the friends who've got nice houses, and they've got fine, healthy children and cats and dogs. You have a crappy apartment that doesn't allow pets.

And when you tell them of your loneliness, these friends cry, "Ah, to be young and single! Be glad you're not married! It's terrible!"

And in your mind you're sitting right outside that restaurant again. Your friends have had their turn at the banquet, and gorged themselves until they were sick. And now they tell you that you should be happy you're starving?

Fuck them.

Fuck *them*.

Get up off the steps and walk back into darkness. You will not starve, and you will not fail, not if you keep searching. Don't waste your gold on those who dismiss you, ignore you, take you for granted and belittle your dreams.

The lonely ones will find each other by the heat of their bodies in the cold blackness.

And they will find their love.

About the Authors

Lucy A. Snyder is the Bram Stoker Award-winning author of the novels *Spellbent, Shotgun Sorceress, Switchblade Goddess*, and the collections *Sparks and Shadows, Chimeric Machines*, and *Installing Linux on a Dead Badger*.

Her fiction has been translated into French, Russian, and Japanese. Over 100 of her short stories and poems have appeared in publications and podcasts such as *Pseudopod, Best Horror of the Year, Strange Horizons, Weird Tales, Hellbound Hearts, Dark Faith, Doctor Who Short Trips: Destination Prague, Chiaroscuro, GUD,* and *Lady Churchill's Rosebud Wristlet.* Her erotica has appeared at *Clean Sheets* and *What Lies Beneath* from Circlet Press.

Lucy was born in South Carolina but grew up in San Angelo, Texas. She currently lives in Worthington, Ohio with her husband and occasional co-author Gary A. Braunbeck. You can learn more about her at www.lucysnyder.com.

Kaysee Renee Robichaud lives and writes in Texas, splitting her time between the slow paced sprawl of San Antonio and hustling Houston. Her recent fiction has appeared in *Sex Toys 2* (from Ravenous Romance), *Like A Cunning Plan* (from Circlet Press), and the succubus themed *Seductress: Erotic Tales of Immortal Desire* (from Cleis Press). Her erotic, epic fantasy novella *Unhasping the World Heart* has been released through Twice Told Tales.